ONCE UPON A TIME

Vice Nganga

First published in Great Britain in 2021 by:

Carnelian Heart Publishing Ltd
Suite A
82 James Carter Road
Mildenhall
Suffolk
IP28 7DE
UK

www.carnelianheartpublishing.co.uk

Paperback ISBN 978-1-914287-00-8

Ebook ISBN 978-1-914287-01-5

A CIP catalogue record for this book is available from the British Library.

Editorial team:
Developmental editor – Daniel Mutendi
Copy editor – Samantha Rumbidzai Vazhure

Cover design:
Artwork - Dayzeren and Somberlain
Layout - Rebeca Covers

Typeset by Carnelian Heart Publishing Ltd
Layout and formatting by DanTs Media

Acknowledgments

I would like to express my heartfelt gratitude to my publisher, Samantha Rumbidzai Vazhure at Carnelian Heart Publishing Ltd. for a splendid job and making my dream to become a published author a reality.

I would also like to thank my wife Faith Nganga, my sons Arthur, Chester and Munyaradzi, and my daughters Mukudzei and Vimbai. Their support makes me strong even when my spirit is low.

I dedicate this book to

My parents Andreas and Agnes Nganga
and
My high school teachers at Nyamuroro Kubatana
particularly Mr Richard Gundani.

Chapter 1

Runesu was a village celebrity. The entire community of Mposi knew him as a great hunter. Yes, the greatest hunter of that time. Nobody could dispute that his hunting prowess was above all men of his community despite his young age.

The young hunter had achieved what men far older than him could only dream of. He had killed a warthog during his first session of hunting. Then a leopard and cheetah became his victims, not counting numerous types of game, from kudu, impala, eland, wildebeest to buffalo. He was one man who did his hunting with passion, such that it ended up being his hobby.

One day, Runesu who was never tired of hunting went alone to check the traps he had set the previous day in the forest.

It was scorching hot. A slight hot wind was blowing from the eastern horizon to the west. This wind did nothing to soften the heat of the sun. One would think hell was more like this very day. Runesu was now in the middle of the forest where the singing of birds punctuated sounds of other creatures which were heard here and there. He was alone. Only his hunting weapons were his companions. He was now very far away from home. Not a single aspect of human life except his soul was around. He could not hear cock crows or the sight of smoke fire anywhere nearby. But that did not discourage him.

The young hunter moved from snare to snare. It seemed a dark day, as he had not seen anything on his snares since morning. Now the sun was up, and it was almost noon.

"A forest gives a man who is tired," so goes the Karanga proverb. It is these wise words from the departed elders that gave him hope. Hope keeps a man going. Where there is hope there is encouragement. Where there is encouragement there is success. So, Runesu soldiered on.

Two snares were left now. As he approached one of them, he saw a small animal caught on it. He was filled with enthusiasm. For a number of days, he had not had a decent meal of meat. In fact, he was not a vegetarian by nature. "Vegetables are snakes' shade," he used to tease his friends.

Runesu was quick to examine what animal it was. It was a squirrel. *Ooh my! How did it get caught there?* He exclaimed to himself. Of course, he had been looking forward to seeing a bigger animal in his snare, but elders said, "What the forests give to you, you must thank wholeheartedly so that tomorrow you won't leave the forests empty handed."

The hunter undid the snare, picked up the dead animal. It was still fresh. It seemed it had been caught a few hours ago, probably in the early hours of the morning. He put the carcass of the animal in his skinbag and moved on.

As he was moving, Runesu heard the sound of a trumpet from afar. *This is Gumhai, the chief's messenger*, Runesu thought to himself. Obviously, he is informing villagers of a meeting. The sound was familiar within the entire community of Mposi. They would not mistake it with any other sound. Even toddlers in the villages of Mposi knew how Gumhai blew the trumpet with unforgettable style. There was a family dispute to be settled or some other announcement to be heard at the chief's palace. Parents from all families involved were entitled to present themselves at the chief's palace. Many parents would obey the chief's verdict, except a few who were thick-headed. But the culprits always faced the long arm of the chief's law by a fitting penalty.

Runesu brushed the thought aside and moved on. As he was headed towards his last snare, he noticed *chitsere*, a honey badger had been caught. It was still alive, struggling to free itself. Someone with a kind heart would have helped the poor creature, but not Runesu the hunter. No hunter would free an animal caught on a snare he had set up as a trap for a wild animal to be caught, unless something was wrong with his brains.

Normally, when meat was in abundance at home, rarely would one eat meat of *chitsere*. It was not considered delicious. But when the situation was like it was, nobody had a choice; after all meat was meat, and you could not compare it to mushroom.

The young man withdrew his knobkerrie and struck the beast once on the forehead. He repeated twice, with the animal screaming and groaning with agony at every blow. After the last blow, life ran out of the poor creature's body. Runesu picked it up and threw it in his skinbag. Now blood was oozing from the skinbag flowing down his legs. He did not care, so he made a U-turn and started walking home.

Runesu walked for more than an hour, navigating his way with sharp instincts. He knew his way home even in the darkness. As he journeyed along, he started singing a hunter's song:

"When a lion refuses to eat grass
It's not pride
That's how it was created
When a lion refuses to eat grass
It's not pride
But that's how it is *hooo iye iye iye wooo*."

Runesu nodded his head in correspondence with the song. Here and there, he would punctuate the song with a high-pitched whistle.

When he was within the village proximity, he bumped into Gwenzi and Toindepi, two of his friends. They had grown up together from infants, to toddlers, to boys who herded goats. They had all subsequently graduated from herding goats to herding cattle together.

Gwenzi was carrying a bundle of reeds on his right shoulder. He was a fishmonger by trade. These reeds were for making *duvu*, a certain bait made out of reeds. It would be laid in shallow waters where fish frequently bred. Once fish entered the inside of the bait, it was impossible for them to come out.

Toindepi was a blacksmith. He was the maker of many kinds of wares of steel and iron, from hoes, knives, spears, arrows, axes and so forth. He would do barter trade with villagers for anything, from farm produce to livestock.

"Greetings Murambwi, the great hunter." Gwenzi and Toindepi greeted Runesu.

"Greetings Samaita. Greetings Mhofu." Runesu replied.

All men greeted each other by totem. Runesu was Murambwi of the lion totem. Gwenzi was Samaita of the zebra totem, while Toindepi was Mhofu of the eland totem.

"How are you, great hunter?"

"I am well, as you can see guys, but the forests are dark."

"Don't say that. How can you say the forests are dark when there is something in your skinbag? Isn't it that the elders say you must be grateful to the forests even if they give you a small thing, so that tomorrow you get exactly what you desire?" Gwenzi reminded him.

"Ooh yes. Thank you, my friend." Runesu responded. He was a generous young man, so he gave the *chitsere* carcass to his two friends to share.

"Do you mind *chitsere* meat?"

"No, we don't mind. Thank you Runesu. Game meat is delicious. For a while now, I have not eaten it." Gwenzi said with excitement.

"Me too. I like meat of any wild animal, be it zebra, monkey or jackal." Toindepi joked. They all laughed. Toindepi was always a jovial man. With him around, there was laughter all day long.

"So, tell us; what are you left with? You can't give all of your meat to us."

Runesu showed them the carcass of *shindi*, a squirrel.

"But it's too small my man."

"It's okay with me. Don't worry. Isn't it the elders say a relationship is half complete until it's fulfilled by food?"

"Ooh yes." Runesu stabbed the earth with his spear, leaving it standing vertically to ease his stance.

"Guys, don't forget that tomorrow is *Chisi*, the third day of the week. Are we ready for our schedule?" Runesu inquired.

"Very much Runesu. I was about to remind you as well." Gwenzi said.

"I shall be the first one to set foot in your homesteads and demand your presence. We don't want men who behave like women. For if you are going on a journey with a woman and you need to leave home at dawn, you have to wake her up before the first cock crows, lest you become late." Toindepi joked.

They all laughed again.

"It's okay guys. Greet your elders for me at home."

With these words, they went separate ways.

Of the three friends, Runesu was the eldest. He was a year older than both Gwenzi and Toindepi. Gwenzi and Toindepi were of the same year with Toindepi being the elder, five months separating their ages.

Gwenzi was married and had one kid. His wife was expecting a second child. Toindepi was also married. He had one child who was older than Gwenzi's. But his wife had not had a second child. "Her womb has a natural contraceptive," villagers maintained. "You don't keep a single child without having a sibling for him or her", even his parents and relatives concurred.

Runesu was still single. He had not secured someone to call a wife. It was this thought of his singleness that bothered his parents. Singleness was something that was scoffed at in Karanga societies. A man or woman was not supposed to die single. If a man died single, he would be buried with a female rat in his grave. This rat served to confuse his spirit so that it assumed he was married. No beer of appeasement was brewed for a man who died single. His spirit was not welcome at home. It was left to roam the forests, because if you brought it home and it dwelt on young male members of the family, they too would find it impossible to marry. The same applied to a female member of the family who died single. If you brought her spirit home and it dwelt on young female members, they would not marry.

Runesu's parents knew everything about this long-kept custom and did not want their son to be buried with a female rat in his grave. It was despised by everyone in the entire community of Mposi and even beyond.

If Runesu's parents were planning something to resolve his singleness that he was not aware of, Runesu and his friends were ahead of them.

Chapter 2

Runesu had feelings for Marujata. She was Makoni's daughter. Her father's homestead was in Tseisi village within the same community of Mposi.

Marujata knew Runesu loved her. His *gwevedzi*, intermediator, had spoken to her several times but to no avail. There was an open secret that circulated within the entire community of Mposi. Makoni had married off Marujata to Mufakose when she was five years old. Even Runesu knew about it. Mufakose was a wealthy man in Gokuda village. He had five wives and twenty-one children. His cattle filled two kraals. In addition to that, he had flocks of sheep and goats, as well as a coffle of donkeys. A man's wealth was measured by the number of wives, children and livestock he had. Even his vast fields where he cultivated crops were part of his wealth.

Makoni was a failure in life. The whole community knew about his story. His father had been very rich. When he died, Makoni inherited all his wealth, because he was the only son of the deceased man. But in a short time, he had squandered everything that his father left for him. He was a habitual boozer who had no ambition in life. At first, he had four wives. Three of them divorced him. Now he had only one wife who was an orphan. "She has nowhere else to go, that's why she is still there," villagers said in whispers.

Makoni's homestead had four dilapidated houses. One would think people of that place had long left their home because it was not tidy either. One could smell the stink of poverty as they approached his yard. His barns were ever half-full, even when other villagers were pronouncing a good year.

It was because of this poverty that he had married off his daughter to a rich man, Mufakose, who was almost his age.

Yes, a man does not grow old. A man is as old as he feels while a woman is as old as she looks. A man can marry a younger woman despite their age difference, but it is never vice versa. A man could not marry a woman older than him. Even so a woman five or less years younger than her husband was considered too old. Everyone in all villages of Mposi was aware of this. There was no argument about it.

Wednesday, the third day of the week, was the day Runesu and his friends would meet and unfold their plan. They spent the day in their separate trades until the sun was over the mountains in the western horizon. Then Toindepi, as he had promised, went about his friends' homesteads calling each one of them. They gathered at a bushy area towards a footpath that led to a stream from where every woman from Tseisi fetched water. They laid in ambush.

They were there for close to an hour. As they lay down, they heard a sound of a woman singing. They cocked their ears and craned their necks. No, it was Chirichoga, a woman notorious for witchery, who lived in the same village of Gokuda. She was carrying a gourd on her head, singing.

"*Nxaa!* Where is that stinking goon going?" Toindepi whispered. Runesu and Toindepi giggled.

"Guys, stop it! Do you want people to hear us? Stop it at once! Toindepi please stop cracking jokes. This is not the time." Gwenzi cautioned the two lads.

"It's okay man. It's okay," Runesu pacified Gwenzi.

Chirichoga walked past them and went down into the stream. In a short while, she was back balancing her gourd filled with water on her head. She was still singing, but this time, a different song. The young men wondered how Chirichoga, a widow from their village fetched water from a well that was owned by Tseisi villagers. "This woman does not cease to amaze people," they murmured in agreement.

The men were patient enough, because in no time, after Chirichoga had vanished beyond the thicket, along came Marujata, the black beauty with her colourful *mbikiza*, an ancient African skirt. Marujata was barefooted. She walked slowly and seemed not to be in a hurry. Although she came from a poor family, she was proud of her beauty. You could see as she walked that she seemed to be walking on top of eggs. Even turning her neck backwards was of big concern like a rhinoceros. She had a long neck and big eyes that when she was looking at you, she resembled a gazelle.

The men watched her as she walked at a snail's pace downstream to the river. They waited until the coast was clear then followed after her, stealthily. Marujata had no idea of the men's presence. As usual she was humming a certain familiar tune. All men knew it, as it was sung during *jenaguru*, the full moon festival.

The three men got close, almost surrounding her. Marujata was squatting on the river sand adjacent to a *mufuku*, a small well dug on the sandy surface where water trickled from. Toindepi was the first to charge forward. He tip-toed, closing the gap between himself and the unaware Marujata.

Toindepi was a giant of a man, more muscular than both Gwenzi and Runesu. He ran his eyes from place to place, checking his surroundings. He then sprang into the air with the agility of a kangaroo and landed on the sandy ground behind Marujata. The thudding sound shocked Marujata who jumped up and only managed to say, "Maiwee!"

Toindepi suddenly cupped her mouth with his huge hand. The hand covered both her mouth and part of her nose, almost suffocating her. The poor lady struggled for life, but her power could not match that of Toindepi. The two wrestled on the sandy surface for a while. Toindepi was still on her back and did not want Marujata to recognise him.

Then Gwenzi joined in. He had ropes made of tree bark in his hands and he used it to tie Marujata's hands and legs. This happened within a few minutes. Time was not on their side. All this time Runesu was aloof, watching from afar.

Marujata had now given in the fight to free herself. The thought of death visited her. *What are these men doing to me?*

What are they up to? Are they going to slay me? She asked herself so many questions that went unanswered.

Toindepi and Gwenzi did not care. All they wanted was to accomplish their mission. They lifted the lady like two men lifting a log, with Toindepi holding the upper part of her body and Gwenzi the hind where her legs were. They vanished into the forest with their load. Runesu followed from behind.

It was now dark. Every homestead was alive in Gokuda village, with clouds of smoke billowing into the sky to offend its peace. Every woman and her daughters were busy preparing food for supper.

Runesu's father was popularly known as Chivi, a clan name. In Karanga culture, one son has to be called by a clan name. Chivi had three wives. Just like any other man within the community, he was a polygamist, and it was as usual as the blue sky one stared at every morning.

Runesu's mother was *vahosi*, the first wife. The two other wives reported to her before they summoned the highest office, which was his father. His mother deputised his father in that order.

Runesu was the eldest son in a family of eight siblings. He had two brothers, one alive, and the other who had died from a crocodile bite. Actually, they had gone fishing with other boys of his age when fate struck. The giant reptile had appeared from nowhere and caught him by the leg, dragging him into the waters of the river. The other boys were bold enough to fight the dangerous reptile, thereby putting their own lives on the line. They eventually won, took their friend home with one leg amputated, blood oozing profusely as they went. Two days later the poor boy died of loss of blood.

Now, seven children of Chivi and his senior wife were alive. Of the five daughters, three were married and lived with their husbands' people. There were other children too from Chivi's other wives.

They had supper in Chivi's homestead before the three men arrived. Just after supper they appeared. Very few members of the extended family saw them. Word had circulated in the family that it was going to be a special day. A day to be merry. The preparations had started in the morning. The hut that would house their visitor had been prepared. Red and dark brown earth were brought from different sources. Patterns were drawn on the inside and outside walls. In the family, there was always an excellent architect, designer, potter and craftsman. The floors of all huts were re-done with cow dung, smoothly leaving a harmless familiar smell.

The three men dashed into the hut that was prepared for the bride. There, a handful of women welcomed them with a common song.

"Muroora tauya naye.
Muroora tauya naye.
Tauya naye nemagumbeze!"

This literally meant we have brought the bride with all necessary clothes.

It was then that it dawned in Marujata's head that she had been done a *musengabere*, a marriage method where the groom and his friends force-marched the bride to his family without her consent. Once there, she was not allowed to flee. If she tried and succeeded, her family would not allow her back home. No family ever took back a daughter force-marched into marriage. Even if they did accept her, her dignity would have been tarnished already. No man would marry her in future. Wherever she went, they would say, "There is that lady who was made a wife by some man and later fled." To the entire village or community, she would be viewed as a brat who broke their custom by giving away her virginity to a man without her parents getting anything. The parents would also be despised for having failed to bring up their daughter in the good ways of their people. Mothers and aunts were especially found wanting. Marujata knew this very well.

The women sat Marujata on a decorated stretcher. They dressed her, first smearing her body with the most valuable oils. They put a headgear on her head and clothed her in all white.

The adornments came from faraway in the Eastern borders, where people called *maPutukezi* (Portuguese) barter traded them with African wares. Nobody had ever seen these *maPutukezi*. It was like a folk story told to kids by an old grandmother before a night fire.

Chapter 3

To many people in the community of Mposi, Chibadura was a nuisance of the society. He was now middle aged, but still unmarried. He had no known children. The only place he called home was where he was born and brought up. His parents had passed on a long time ago. All his other siblings were married and had their homes and families across the community. Other men and women of his age had brought pride to their families and the entire community by attaining certain achievements, but not Chibadura, a man of no self-esteem and no ambition. He was often drunk, roaming from one household that had beer to another. He was notorious for leaving such places when the drums had gone silent, and every gourd of beer empty. Villagers no longer laughed at him. They had laughed at him in the beginning, but they ended up realising that it was a sheer waste of time and energy. Chibadura would not show an aorta of affection.

No man is bad right through, so goes the Karanga proverb. Chibadura was the best drummer the entire community had ever had. On special occasions, one would easily see why he was never absent. He would beat the drums with zeal and artistry that left everyone in awe and applauding.

Marujata heard the drums and guessed well who the drummer was, for nearly everyone in the community knew Chibadura.

The drums beat until midnight. The morale was now high. A combination of dust and smoke from the dance arena could be seen high in the sky. Lead vocalists churned song after song, with Chibadura beating the drums accordingly, with unforgotten skill.

Then there was a time for presents. The bride was brought before the crowd of relatives and neighbours. Her face was covered. A little fortune had to be paid, for one to be granted an opportunity to see her face.

"Why did Runesu do this? Bringing an ape of a woman and calling her a wife?" One aunt jokingly said.

"Ooh she is very beautiful, like a mermaid. Such beauty is associated with witches!"

Another grandmother teased her.

"Look at the cracks on her feet. She looks like someone who stepped on sacred graves." A neighbour said amid laughter from the crowd.

Marujata knew her people's customs very well, such that all words mouthed did not anger her. She had been brought up amongst her people, having attended many such marriage ceremonies. Other girls and she had also said nasty words to other brides during these ceremonies. Now it was her turn to be mocked.

Presents of kitchenware showered the event. Baskets, mats, cloths, clay pots, wooden plates, gourds, beads and oils were some of the gifts she received.

The following day, Runesu was awakened by a stray bull which had broken into their cattle kraal. It was Ziyambi's bull. Ziyambi was a fellow neighbour. He was shocked to see that it was still dark with the *hweva*, morning star shining brightly from the east. It was like the star had taken up the chieftainship where there was no moon nor sun.

Runesu went straight to his father's cattle kraal. When he saw the notorious bull, he quickly knew the kraal wall was broken somewhere. He searched the whole perimeter of the kraal until he found the aperture. He took the logs that lay carelessly by the kraal side and mended the hole to perfection. He did not drive away the bull, because driving it away would be a sheer waste of time. He knew it would still come back and cause more damage to the kraal.

After that, Runesu walked home whistling. Anyone could recognise that it was a whistle of joy.

"Hey, whose child is that one, who whistles at night?" A voice spoke from a nearby path leading to the fields.

"Ooh, it's Chirichoga. Good morning old lady."

"*Eee* stop it! What is good about this night you call morning? Is that the reason why you blow a whistle like that? Didn't your parents tell you, if you whistle at night witches will answer you?"

"I thought it was already morning, old lady."

"Ooh morning, really? What morning with no red rays of the sun on the eastern horizon? What morning is that?"

"I am sorry old lady. I didn't mean to disrespect you or any adult."

"Okay then, go your way and never do it again."

"Sure, old lady. "

Chirichoga left. Runesu stood there wondering where the old lady was going, since it was night-time as she had said. *That's why people say she is a witch. Where is she going alone during this time?* Runesu could not understand.

Marujata, as the new bride, woke up earlier than anyone else in the homestead. She woke Runesu's sister, Chezhira, so that she could show her where things were, as she went about doing her morning chores. Chezhira knew where brooms were kept, where trash should be disposed, and she would lead the path to the village well.

As a new bride, it was considered immoral to wake up late. Marujata knew it, having memorised the entire oral syllabus of adulthood that her aunts and mother at home always recited with much emphasis. She took the biggest of all brooms and swept the whole yard, making heaps of rubbish here and there. In no time, she was done. But she did not collect the rubbish for disposal. Her mother and aunts had told her what must be done.

When other family members woke up, they found Marujata rooted on one spot with her broom. She had stood there for a while like she did not exist, motionless like a statue. They all paid her in kind, as was customary, and that was when she carried on with her duties. She went to the well. When they came back, Chezhira brought her gourd down when they got into the yard, but Marujata stood stuck on one spot again without saying a word. Her gourd was still on her head. The family paid in kind again. She filled all the water gourds she found in the cooking hut. After that, she made fire. The sun was now rising from the eastern horizon with sharp rays that signalled a hot day.

Marujata put a pot of water on the fire and brought it to warmth. She gave each member of the family, including children, water for bathing.

Runesu's mother brought a calabash of *maheu,* a fermented drink made from mealie-meal and malt. She also brought *mutakura,* a mixture of cooked maize seed and round nuts. They ate together, women scooping from one plate. Men had their own plate, and children theirs, each group according to age and gender. As for *maheu* they would take turns sipping the sour liquid each. Men, women and children had their separate calabash each. And behold, it was good when relatives sat down for food.

The eating would be interrupted here and there as a passer-by could greet them and they would invite him or her to the food table which he or she would no doubt decline, but in a polite manner. Some would say they were full when in actual fact they were hungry. Only an insane adult would turn to any home for food. But customarily passers-by were invited to eat, even when one knew they would not accept the invitation. All one had to do was to fulfil the formality.

After breakfast, Marujata went to a nearby bush to fetch firewood. She was accompanied by Chezhira, as before.

Chezhira was several moons younger than Marujata, but she understood every chore any woman of her age knew. Her mother, just like any other mother could have done, had brought up her daughter in ways of their people.

The name Chezhira was given to her by a certain aunt who was married in a distant village. Her mother was heavy with the pregnancy that brought her into the world. Everyone had gone to the fields except for the two of them. Chezhira's mother started to feel some labour pains. She was not certain the baby's time had arrived. They then decided to go to the home of a certain midwife. They failed to reach the midwife's place in time. Her aunt dragged her mother into a nearby bush. It was that bush that served as a maternity ward, and the baby was born with the help of the aunt. Ooh yes, the baby was called Chezhira because she was born by the roadside. The name was not only for identification purposes. It served as a constant reminder of some family history as well.

The two ladies made two heaps of firewood, each tying the wood with tree barks. Marujata had the bigger and longer *svinga*, bundle. They made a round small mat out of tree leaves each. The *hata* was used on one's head to ease carrying of the firewood. They carried the firewood heading home, Chezhira leading the way, Marujata following behind in single file.

When they got home, Chezhira dropped her bundle on the ground. Marujata did not. She stood there balancing her bundle on her head. Members of the family paid handsomely. She then dropped her bundle of firewood.

"Tete, you don't leave your bundle tied like that. It's sacred, don't you know?"

"Ooh dear, what will happen if I leave the bundle like that?"

"When you get abducted, you will spend the whole night tied. Your abductors won't free you."

"Ooh my... let me untie the bundle. Spending the whole night with my hands cuffed? No."

Chapter 4

Marujata's mother had been the first wife, way back when her husband Makoni had many wives. Now the other three wives had gone back to their people. She was the only one left, probably because she had nowhere to go. Her parents had passed on when she was very young. Barely could she remember their faces. She had married Makoni when she was a young girl. Because she did not know the exact year she was born, villagers and her relatives assumed that she was a girl of fifteen years then, judging by seeing girls whom they said were of her age group as they grew up.

The other three wives left all their children with their father, so Marujata's mother was mother to all twelve of them.

Makoni and Marujata's mother had five children, two girls and three boys. The other seven children were Marujata's half-sisters and half-brothers. She was the second born child. Her brother Tanaka was the firstborn child, then followed two boys and a girl being the lastborn child.

"Tanaka! Tanaka, can't you hear me?"

"*Mhaa!*" Tanaka replied from beyond one of the houses. He was busy sharpening his spear. A friend had invited him for a night hunt. There were wild pigs terrorising villagers by destroying their gardens at the riverbanks, so the boys wanted to ambush them and make them meat for consumption.

"Tanaka! Am I talking to myself?" Gambiza, for that was her name, beckoned to him.

"Come here."

"Good evening, *mhai*. Did you just call me?"

"Yes Tanaka. Call your brothers. Look, since I sent Marujata to the well some hours ago she is nowhere to be seen. What on earth has eaten her in this world where people roam peacefully?"

Tanaka did not reply. He knew what had to be done. His father was not at home, as usual, having gone to look for booze in the neighbourhood. Tanaka called his two young brothers Zvidzai and Matenda. He narrated the story word for word, as he had heard it from his mother. Tanaka was arming himself as he spoke. He had his spear already. He took a number of arrows and his bow. A knobkerrie was tied on his waist.

Zvidzai took his spear, bow and arrows in the same fashion as his brother Tanaka. Matenda, the youngest but tallest of the three, also got armed the same way, only that his weapons were smaller in make than his brothers'. Yes, they suited the body that carried them. They took off. One would think they were going to fight a dangerous enemy. They moved in single file from the yard, straight into the footpath that led to the stream where the village well was.

Gambiza watched as her sons left. She was left bemused with both hands akimbo. She stood there for a while until Sekai, her stepdaughter startled her.

"Good evening *mhai*." Gambiza did not reply. Sekai knew at once that something was not alright with her stepmother. She was one such person who could not hide her emotions. She was not a good pretender. Whenever she tried hard to conceal her emotions something betrayed her, maybe her conscience.

"Mother are you okay? Is something troubling you?"

"Don't worry Sekai I shall be alright. It's not something that should bother you." As usual, she failed dismally in her effort to hide her anxiety.

"Will you please make fire for me?"

"Yes, mother but not before you tell me what's troubling you. I may not be of help mother, but telling me will help. Isn't it what our people say, a problem said is half solved?"

Gambiza ran a hand on her hair from the front scalp to the back of her head. She was not at liberty with her soul.

"Sekai, my heart is not at peace. I sent your sister Marujata to fetch water at the well exactly at the same time you and your friend Punha went to fetch firewood. But until now she has not come back yet. Can you tell me where she has gone?"

Sekai was all ears, listening with the attentiveness of a hunter stalking game. Sure, it was unusual for Marujata or any girl in their village, to be outdoors at that time of the day.

"So, I have sent your brothers to go look for her." Gambiza continued with no answer from Sekai. She was wide-mouthed all this time as her stepmother explained.

In single file, the three young men were now approaching the stream. They were all silent. Only the rattling of their weapons against their bodies and sometimes against shrubs that were along the pathway on both sides, could be heard. The other sounds, apart from nocturnal sounds from the bushes, were the stretching of their muscles, footsteps and their heartbeats. Dusk was rolling on now, but it was not dark yet.

Ahead of them was the village well, deserted. It was not surprising why no woman was there. Time was up for such errands from any sensible woman who valued her womanhood. The young men stood there confused, taken aback. With the little light left before it was completely dark, they moved a little backwards by the riverbank where there was more clay than sand. Tanaka knelt down and examined the ground for Marujata's footprints.

"Yes, these are her footprints! I know them from a single glance." Zvidzai came near, knelt on one leg with the other one, which he supported with the weight of his body.

"Yes, they're hers. Those are Marujata's footprints. But see brother, there are other footprints too. Too big to be women's footprints."

Tanaka came to where Zvidzai knelt. Sure, there were far too many footprints around the well, with some deformed, one would think someone was dancing on the muddy surface.

Matenda who was guarding the place like a king's watchman, started walking around the place, spear held in a ready stance. Their father had told them, "when men are examining something in a forest, they don't all participate at once. Just like baboons do when invading a field of maize, one has to be the watchman, lest you are all caught unaware by an enemy."

"Brother!"

"Yes."

"This is Marujata's gourd." Tanaka and Zvidzai jumped to Matenda's announcement.

"And her cup!"

Tanaka picked the two pieces of the gourd and examined them. Yes, the gourd belonged to their sister. How did she break it? Was something or someone after her? Tanaka pondered silently. Zvidzai picked up the cup made of the same gourd plant. Yes, it was her sister's cup.

"Thank you Matenda, take to your position or else enemies will pounce on us unexpectedly."

No one could make heads or tails of the confusion. Where was their sister? What had happened to her? Whose footprints were those? All these questions, yearning for answers, hung over them with no single answer to any of them.

After searching everywhere around the well, with no sign of their sister's presence, the boys returned home. They looked like men coming from a funeral of a relative who had died unexpectedly and mysteriously. Tanaka was pondering how he would relate the news to his mother without scaring her. Gambiza was a woman of light heart. A small issue would bring her to tears. At village funerals, she was known for being the loudest crier. Even consoling her was not easy.

As they approached their homestead, they heard the sound of drums beating in the opposite direction. That was towards Gokuda village, beyond Gambure river. They did not bother finding out what the drum beatings were for, because they were buried in thoughts about the whereabouts of their sister.

When Tanaka and his young brothers came back home, their father Makoni was not yet home. Within a short period, word had gone viral in Makoni's homestead and the entire neighbourhood, that Marujata was nowhere to be seen.

In the morning of the following day, many versions of the story of Marujata's missing were heard. Some said Mufakose had taken his wife, after impatiently waiting for donkey years without his in-laws giving her to him, as per custom. Others said they saw her with a boy from another village. He must be the one who snatched her. Still, others maintained that she had eloped to a man from a faraway village. Such were village rumours. Some people would speak as if they were there when Marujata disappeared.

Makoni was the last person to know that Marujata had disappeared. His sister who was married in Masarira, a village to the north of Gokuda village paid him a visit after she got wind of Marujata's missing. Her mother Gambiza had sent Matenda to inform their aunt about it.

Makoni was not an easy man to confront with dreadful news, especially when the occasion pointed someone as an offender. In most cases, one would need a counsel of the whole clan to persuade him to listen.

"Which Marujata are you talking about, sister?" Makoni had coolly asked. But his question had that venomous taste of a cobra striking an impala.

"Which other Marujata can we talk about, who is not our daughter?" Aunt Manyati said, staring straight into her brother's face.

"Have you answered me then?"

"Yes, I did."

"Listen dear sister, if where you are married you are rude to your husband and his people, please don't come and do it here in my homestead, lest you step on a viper's head."

Gambiza was seated far away, as if she was not part of the discussion. The other members of the Makoni family were also there, the entire extended family.

"This child has made fire in our eyes." Gambiza murmured to herself.

"Brother, this is a word I received this morning, and I did the rightful thing, according to custom. I called all of you to hear this, so that no one of you will say I heard the news with one ear. My question is, am I being rude when my brother's daughter goes missing and I as aunt call for a family meeting?"

Makoni's cousin brother made a sigh of relief and asked for a cup of water, although it was still in the morning. He was given the water and drank with noisy gulps. He put away the empty cup and began talking.

"Excuse me, *vaera* Nyati." It was a salutation of their totem. He continued.

"I don't see where aunt Manyati has gone wrong. It is the custom of our people that if a daughter goes missing in a homestead, an aunt is the rightful person to inform her brother."

He stopped talking. Everyone wondered whether it was a pause or full stop, until a certain period of time passed without him continuing.

"Of all my daughters, any of them can elope to any man of their choice. I don't have a problem with that, except Marujata. Who doesn't know Marujata is Mufakose's wife? What man can dare snatch someone's wife in broad daylight? What bravery is that? Is that not a crime?"

"Ooh yes, it is." They all agreed.

Chapter 5

Two weeks had passed and Marujata was now the new daughter-in-law in Chivi's homestead. She was now getting used to life in a different family. Ever since she was born, she had never been away from her family, except on a few occasions when she seldom visited her aunts.

The day was Sunday, the last day of the week. The following night, she was going to be presented to her husband. For the first time, the two were going to share a room over night as husband and wife.

Runesu's grandfather, the father to his father, had passed on some years ago. They said war broke out between their people and the Barwe people of the north. Just like other men he was not lucky on that particular day. He died from a spear stab on his chest that tore his rib cage piercing his heart. This happened when Runesu was still a little boy.

Runesu's grandmother was still alive, probably one of the oldest women in the village. She walked straight with no aid of a walking stick. It was because she was short. Tall people bend their backs earlier than short ones, villagers said.

She was the only source of folk stories in the family. A great entertainer at the fall of night before a bonfire. All the little children liked her. Now she had seen grandchildren and great grandchildren, but it was Runesu's marriage that made her happiest. That day in the evening when the sun was almost on the mountain tops in the west, she went into Runesu's hut. Inside, there was nothing except for a reed bed. She prepared the bed afresh putting a white cloth on top. Then she put a blanket made of jackal hide, smoothened by an excellent craftsman. After making sure that all was well, she left, closing the door behind her.

The following day in the morning, Marujata woke up earlier than everyone in the family. She started doing her chores as usual. Grandmother Chinjanja also woke up early.

She walked across the yard to the *bakwa*, where firewood was kept. There, in the midst of the yard, she met Marujata who knelt down on both knees and saluted the old woman. She then continued on her way. As she passed, Chinjanja looked back to watch her stride. Yes, she seemed to walk with a slight limp. The old woman smiled to herself. She went straight to Runesu's hut and knocked. Runesu answered amid a yawn.

"Please wake up and go milk the cows. I need milk now, my grandchild."

"Grandma so early, why?"

"When elders order you to do a task, do you ask why? Do you think you are still a baby? Continue behaving like a spoilt boy and this beautiful daughter of Makoni will run away from you."

Runesu laughed as he opened the door.

"Run away from me to where?"

"Either to her people or to another man's home."

"Abomination."

"Fine, it would be an abomination. But every wrong done is appeased."

"Grandmother, don't talk like that. You know how hard I worked to get this lady. You break my heart. Don't tell me you are serious."

Chinjanja laughed. Actually, the two were the best of friends.

Runesu went into the cooking room, fetched water with a cup and washed his face. He then took all the milking utensils and headed for the cattle kraal. Chinjanja watched him as he went, until he vanished beyond her sight.

After Runesu had gone to the cattle kraal, Chinjanja went into his hut, removed the blanket on the reed bed and took away the white cloth that was covering the mattress made out of feathers. She examined the cloth. It was smeared with blood on the centre. The old woman smiled as she folded the cloth. *You don't mistake a red substance on a white background.* She got out of the hut and headed to her hut where other women were waiting for her. She did not say a word as she entered the hut. She just unfolded the cloth for everyone to see for themselves.

The other women looked with curiosity as the cloth was unfolded. The big red spot caught the attention of all. They all started ululating and shouting.

"Yes, she was a true virgin. Thank you Makoni people. Your daughter is the jewel of the community! She was brought up in ways of our people!"

One would think the Makoni people were present. The noise alerted men of the family who came as the women walked out of Chinjanja's hut. Some joined the jubilation, but old men remained seated, smiling and talking in low voices.

News that Marujata had eloped to a certain man's homestead when everybody knew she was married off to Mufakose swept across the whole community. Even in Mufakose's homestead, it became public news.

"If a man who has five wives decides to marry a sixth one, is he saying he is not satisfied with all his wives? Is he saying all five are not wife enough to quench his lust?"

Mufakose's second wife said. All the other women laughed.

"But if Mufakose had paid Makoni the *rovora* in full, what was that daughter of Makoni doing in her father's homestead? It's like you go and buy a commodity from the marketplace, then leave it behind. Suppose you come back and the seller starts telling you stories after using what you gave him as payment, which he or she can neither refund."

A third wife said.

"Why was he taking a sixth wife when we here are not being adequately provided for?" This was the fifth wife.

"All of you keep quiet! Five wives or six wives, what's the difference? If you wanted a monogamy, why did you marry him? Didn't you know he had a wife or wives already? Stupid women!" Mai Simba, Mufakose's senior wife shouted at the junior wives.

"Mai Simba, don't tell us we are stupid. It's you who is stupid. You were married first. Why did your husband go on to marry four more wives during your presence? Are you not wife material?" This was Chihera spitting venom straight into Mai Simba's face. She was the only woman the senior wife dreaded. When she married Mufakose, she had made it known that the reason she was in his homestead was because of him only, not any other woman. She was the wife to this man, not any woman who was a co-wife like herself. Even Mufakose had tried his level best to tame her but failed by all skills applied.

Manjenjenje the fifth wife, youngest of them all, as cool and harmless as a dove, was quiet all this time. She seemed to enjoy the noisy talk of these women.

"Shut up all of you!" Mufakose had arrived without anyone noticing him.

"Each to her house! Are you all having a meeting to kill me? Now listen, you have stalked an alert one. Today I won't eat anything from your dishes."

"You will die of hunger master. Hunger has no respect even for a grownup man." Chihera spoke almost in a whisper.

"I said shut up Chihera! You don't open your filthy cave when the authority of this yard is talking. Neither do you cough or sneeze when a man who gave your father twelve heads of cattle for *rovora* is talking. When you hear this voice from any quarter of this yard, you calm down as a sign of submission and loyalty."

Chihera as usual would not listen. She kept on mumbling something as they all dispersed.

Mufakose walked past the yard to his house where he took an adze and headed to the kraal. His unfinished yoke was waiting for him. He was to do the final touches to it. As he was about to leave the yard, a male voice stopped him.

"Ooh Mhofu, the male eland!"

"The male eland is here. Welcome Jekanyika my good friend." After greetings, Mufakose gave his friend a stool to sit on. They found a quiet place and sat down. Jekanyika often paid him a visit as he used to do to him, but not in these hours of the morning. Mufakose knew something was amiss. "If you see a friend visiting you during a hailstorm, it means the news he carries is very important. He has seen it not well to wait for the hailstorm to pass, so that he leaves the comfort of his homestead unhindered."

"A hailstorm is nothing when a word of information must reach a friend in time. What if the hailstorm goes on until dusk?" Jekanyika replied.

"I am all ears my friend." Mufakose interjected.

Jekanyika paused for a while, as if to find enough energy to begin his story. He coughed to clear his throat and fidgeted on his stool.

"I am cock sure this story circulating in our village has reached your ears."

"Which story?"

"Haven't you heard that your wife, Makoni's daughter eloped to another man's place?"

Mufakose looked aside as if he was not interested. He brought out his snuff horn from his skinbag and opened it, drained a little snuff and plucked it in both nostrils and breathed in. He sneezed heavily and a tear ran down his cheek. He rubbed it with the back of his palm.

"All I know is that Marujata is my wife. The man who took her away is a thief. What he did is a crime. Our people know that. You know that. He knows that. Even Marujata is not ignorant of that."

"Sure. So, what are you going to do?" Jekanyika asked with his right hand striking the ground with his walking stick.

"Look Jekanyika, these are rumours. But where there is smoke there is bound to be fire. I will wait to hear from them. It's obvious the rumours started in Makoni's homestead after his daughter went missing. So, should he keep quiet without notifying me about such a serious offence?"

"I don't think so. But there is something that I heard." Jekanyika added.

"What is it?" Mufakose sat upright with renewed curiosity.

"Just last week there was some drum beating of welcoming a bride in the family somewhere at the end of this village." Jekanyika pointed in the direction.

"And what about that?"

"I heard that she was the one who was being received by that man's people."

"Jekanyika, don't tell me you are serious. A man from this village snatching my wife? This is an open declaration of war with me. Over my dead body will I allow that to happen. I am not going to wait for Makoni. I will hunt down the stupid coward woman grabber." Mufakose clenched his fists. Anger was choking him.

"Calm down my friend. Elders say don't rush to swallow when chewing is still needed. Let's find out to which homestead was your wife taken. Once we know which people took her, then we know from where to start."

Mufakose listened quietly. If there was a man who could be listened to by Mufakose even when he was angry, it was Jekanyika. Mufakose's wives often sought refuge in his homestead after a quarrel with their husband. The two friends agreed to meet the following day and map a way of finding out who had taken Marujata. At least Jekanyika had unveiled a clue.

Gokuda village stretched from the east to the west along a range of hills. It ran parallel to a stream, Gambure which is a tributary of Mwenezi river. Tseisi village was situated beyond this stream. Both villages fetched water from the same stream, but they had different wells. Even those of the same village often had different wells depending on their geographical location. Those situated at the far eastern end had their own wells. Those in the middle had theirs. Those at the western end also had their own. Mufakose's homestead was on the eastern end, while Chivi's homestead was on the western end. Rarely would these villagers meet, unless when the kraal-head called for a meeting of the entire village, or they would meet for *jenaguru,* full moon festivals. Other small gatherings like farming cooperatives and marriage celebrations were done separately. One would think they were people of different villages.

Mufakose and Jekanyika knew the well that belonged to those of the western end. They also knew Marujata as a new daughter-in-law would come and fetch water.

Chapter 6

Gokuda village had two nuisances, Makoni and Bopoto. These were men of no ambitions, no self-esteem, no dignity. It seemed Bopoto was worse than Makoni. Makoni had a wife and children. He was rarely arraigned before the village headman for any offence, whereas Bopoto was always seen there. Not a month passed without him being accused of something. He was also a habitual liar who had the audacity to deny what was in his hand and say he did not touch it.

Of all his offences that he was convicted before the headman's court, four stood out. On one occasion he had castrated Mhizha's bull, which was used as an ancestral deity. On another occasion, he had ambushed women from Tseisi village at their bath place by the stream. While they were busy bathing, his eyes were feasting on their naked bodies. On a separate occasion, he was found in a pigsty having sex with a sow. In another instance, he had told Mai Simba, Mufakose's senior wife, that she was a witch.

"I caught her at the village graveyard eating the corpse of my father one night. This other day I saw her smearing blood on our doorstep," Bopoto had elaborated. *Where was he coming from when he saw Mai Simba doing such evil things*, villagers wondered.

For all these offences, his mother had paid fines on his behalf. One would think he would reconsider his deeds and repent, alas he continued with no shame. He even had no pity for his mother who was a widow.

One day, he was accused of molesting a girl at the village well. He had shamelessly smooched her breasts without her consent. This act, according to Karanga culture, was tantamount to rape. As usual, Bopoto's mother was asked to pay compensation on his behalf. The old woman refused this time around.

"Headman, Bopoto is not a boy anymore. He is a man. Being unmarried does not mean he is an infant, actually it's his cowardice that made him remain single when boys far younger than him have wives and children. If I continue paying fines for him, do you think he will leave his bad ways and repent? No, he won't because these fines do not pain him since they are not from his hard-earned resources."

The entire court of elders agreed that the old woman had spoken well, Bopoto was spoilt. They adjourned the court after agreeing that they would find a suitable fine for Bopoto, a shell of a man who wanted to give villagers sleepless nights.

When Bopoto got home, he accused his mother of humiliating him at the headman's court. His mother still emphasised her word, that nothing would come from her homestead to pay for his fine. A quarrel broke. Bopoto slapped his mother. The old woman fought back. With her lesser power, she bit his arm until he groaned like a dying helpless lion. When he was eventually freed, blood oozing from the wound, he swiftly ran for something to revenge with. He came back brandishing a whip, with which he whipped his mother until neighbours came and rescued the poor old woman.

Bopoto's uncles came in the morning of the following day. Both sets of uncles from his paternal and maternal sides sat for a family meeting. Bopoto's offence was talked over. His maternal uncles said he was supposed to perform what is known as *kutanda botso*, appeasing the spirit of his maternal lineage. Failure to do so, if his mother were to die without such appeasement, evil omens would haunt him for the rest of his life. He would know no peace, they maintained.

The following day, they dressed their nephew in animal hides of all kinds of animals that were considered bad and threw ashes on his body then force-marched him along the footpath that cut through the length of the village, shouting,

"Here is the fool that beat his mother!"
"Here is the fool that beat his mother!"

They entered every homestead. Bopoto had a wooden plate and a big skinbag for begging. At every homestead they entered they gave him a plateful of either millet or rapoko, but not before they scowled at him shouting, "Stupid mother beater. Useless parent beater. May your mother's spirit haunt you if you don't repent!"

As they moved the procession grew longer. The shouting became louder from different voices. In some homesteads they spat on his face. Others smeared mucus, threw ashes and soil on his body.

When the skinbag was full, they did not help him carry it. In fact, they pushed him forward and said, "Move mother beater. Move, we have no mercy for such a foolish parent beater."

The millet and rapoko was used to brew beer to appease the spirit of his maternal lineage. It was only after the beer drinking that he was freed. Still, villagers, his relatives and neighbours could not believe Bopoto was a changed man.

The procession that followed Bopoto interrupted the Chivis' schedule. However, they allowed the group to come into their homestead as was the custom of their people. After the crowd had gone, they resumed their resolution.

Two days before, the Chivi family had sent a *munyai*, go-between to Makoni to inform them that if they were looking for their daughter, they should not look for her anywhere else but in Chivi's homestead. The go-between came back running and narrated a story of sorrow where he said he had escaped death by a whisker. The Makonis were after his life.

A second go-between was sent after the first one told the Chivis that he could not continue with the job. It was this second man who came back with a bruised leg, limping. They had set dogs on him and chased him away. They had no discussion with thugs who came under the cover of darkness to steal their daughter who was someone's wife for that matter, they openly told him.

When two families were locked in such a disagreement, which seemed unsolvable, then a third party had to intervene.

Makoni had no known friend. The only person who was close to him was Taruvona. Even so, the two could not be called friends. Yes, they had a few things in common. Taruvona had a small family, a wife and three children. Villagers said they were not his biological children. Taruvona's young brother had slept with Taruvona's wife on every occasion she was said to be pregnant. Taruvona was impotent and could not father children. For five years, the couple had no children until his parents secretly visited a diviner and were told that it was their son who was barren. In an effort to conceal their son's lameness, they had a secret meeting with his wife during his absence and told her the whole story. They also made it known to Taruvona's young brother. They then convinced the two to be intimate. It was culturally right to do so, and there was no abomination, they emphasized. But one condition was set. Taruvona was never allowed to catch wind of this plan. It was agreed. These were village stories, just as witches and wizards were discussed behind their backs. So, this story did not reach Taruvona's ears.

Taruvona was a drunkard whose appetite for beer was always excellent. He did not mind the brand of beer. Anything called beer, whether good or bad was okay with him. He was the only man in Mposi community who smoked tobacco from a pipe and sniffed snuff with his nose. This combination was unseen and unheard of. A person could either be a pipe smoker or a nose sniffer, not both ways.

It is during these drinking sprees that Makoni and Taruvona seldom met. They would drink together, talking of no productive topics. They both had extreme ambitions that everyone deemed to be unachievable.

"You remember that lion that went berserk and ate our livestock some time ago, if l had the power, I would trap it and put a bell on its neck," Taruvona said one day. Both of them laughed revealing their stained teeth.

"Taruvona, so that wherever the lion goes the bell will ring alerting any creature that can be its prey." Makoni said, praising his friend.

"Yes. And you know what? It will die of hunger."

They drank and puffed tobacco from their pipes.

"Taruvona."

"Yes Makoni."

"Did you hear that Bopoto said Mai Simba is a witch? The same Mai Simba is Mufakose's senior wife. The same Mufakose who is supposed to be my son-in-law. So, Mai Simba and my daughter will live in the same homestead sharing utensils, tools and a husband. Do you see it right?"

"Hmmmm too bad. That's too bad. That's putting your goat in a lion's den."

"But you know, I had already married off my daughter. So, my plan is to wait for a day when that witch invades my property. I will catch her and hammer a wooden peg on her forehead so that when the sun rises every villager will see her."

The two men laughed to tears. Such were their stories. Useless and meaningless stories of nonsense.

It was this Taruvona whom the Chivis thought of. They wanted him to be their go-between since they had seen Taruvona and Makoni together occasionally. Actually, the Chivis had no option. Of course, they would not trust Taruvona with such delicate matters of the family. Sending Taruvona on such an errand was equal to sending a blindman to go looking for a needle in a skinbag full of other accessories, some members of the family said. Still, they had no other way out. It was becoming uncomfortable to live with someone's daughter without observing marriage rites. Suppose she got sick or some worse calamity happened, how would they inform her people? They were playing with fire. Yes, their actions were saying, "fire you cannot burn me."

Chapter 7

Mufakose was a giant of a man, tall with an imposing figure that would make a coward wet themselves with fear, when confronted by him. His hoarse voice was so bassy, one would not mistake it with any other when he opened his mouth to speak. Age was catching up with him, only that he did not want to show it. But you cannot run away from old age, one part of the inevitable sequence of creation.

Jekanyika had a slender figure with visible veins running all over his body; the lean type that never grew stout even if they lived lavishly. His feet were too big for his body. He genetically inherited them from his father, villagers always teasingly said.

Jekanyika had two wives. He had one wife to begin with. The second was inherited from his brother. His brother had gone missing some time ago. A mermaid who used to be seen at dawn by the banks of river Mwenezi took him away.

"He is residing with the mermaids in the underworld. His people must not cry for his release. But his wife did cry. You see, he will never return because his wife cried." All these words were talk of the village.

After a year without Jekanyika's brother's coming back, the family had a meeting where his wife was told to choose who to marry among one of the male members of the family. Only nephews or young brothers were eligible for choice. Elder brothers to her husband were ineligible because they were considered as fathers, in the event their biological father died. They automatically assumed the role of the father during the real father's absence. So, his brother's wife chose him for a husband. This custom, called *kugara nhaka* in Karanga, where one of the living brothers marries the wife of their deceased brother. That's how Jekanyika sailed in the same boat as polygamous men of the community.

The two men had similar sets of weapons from knobkerries, spears, bows and arrows. They walked for a while without talking to each other, both of them abreast of each other, not really minding who was ahead or behind.

Tapera was Runesu's half-brother, born of Chivi's second wife, Masigwede. Tapera was Masigwede's last born. She had only four children having experienced a number of miscarriages and stillborn babies in-between. Some of her children died in their infancy. How such a single woman recorded the highest infant mortality rate in the village baffled everyone. "How can Chivi fold his hands when evil spirits invade his homestead? He should rise up and go look for a good diviner. Maybe the spirits of his ancestors are angry with him. Or those of his wife want appeasement for a wrong done by her people, who knows," villagers said.

Tapera's name literally meant "we are finished". A Karanga word of lamentation, given to a child after a series of deaths in a family. It was not by sheer coincidence that his name matched all misfortunes that befell his mother.

Being one of the youngest boys of the family it was his duty to herd his father's livestock. They would take turns with his half-brothers to do the herding. This particular day he opened the kraal and joined other herd boys of the village at the grazing field.

In the bushy grazing field, the herd boys played games as their animals grazed. When they were tired, they started looking for wild fruits. They were eating wild berries when two unfamiliar men appeared not far away from them.

"Greetings young man."

"Greetings father. How are you?"

"We are well and hope you are well too."

"I am well father."

They were speaking to one of the herd boys. Tapera was at the furthest end. He kept quiet as his friend continued with the conversation."

"Young man, can we ask you something?"

Pondai the herd boy looked at the two men with wonder.

"Sure father."

"A few days ago, I heard some drum beatings in the direction of your village. They sounded like marriage ceremony drums. Who was having that ceremony?" Jekanyika asked with much curiosity. The boy scratched his kinky hair in thought.

"Father, you know we don't reveal village secrets to strangers."

"But we are not strangers. We are men from the eastern end of this village. Maybe you don't know us, but your elders know us. So, my question is, who had taken a new bride then?"

Pondai stared at the two men with scepticism.

"Ooh, that one? It was in Chivi's homestead. His son Runesu married a new bride. Runesu is brother to Tapera who is over there." He pointed in the direction at which Tapera was standing. After the inquisition, the men thanked Pondai and passed by. When they were gone, Tapera came to Pondai with clenched fists.

"You stupid warthog! Why did you tell them all those things about my family?"

"Tapera, don't call me a warthog! If I am a warthog then you are an ape. A pregnant she-ape. Get away!"

"Pondai, stop calling me names or I will break your brittle skull."

"So, you think while you are breaking my skull, I will be watching you like a patient paying attention to a herbalist smearing remedy on an aching head? You are mad!"

A fight nearly ensued were it not for the other herd boys who came and extinguished the flames of the quarrel before they caused untold harm. After that, each herd boy went his way, back to the berry trees, before rounding their animals to the drinking spot in the stream. Tapera disappeared without telling anyone where he was going. No one bothered to find out what he was up to.

Runesu and his two friends, Toindepi and Gwenzi were in the nearby forest, close to where the boys were herding. They had gone there to harvest honey from *dendende*, certain bee-like insects that made honey, but did not sting like bees did.

They saw Tapera coming with perspiration dripping from all over his body. They quickly saw that something was not right.

"Tapera."

"Yes brother!"

"I can see something is wrong. What brought you here?"

"Brother, some men passed through our grazing field. They asked something about the drum beatings that sounded like a bride celebration." Runesu and his friends listened with gloomy faces.

"How many were there?"

"Two." Tapera raised his right hand with his two fingers up.

"And what did you boys say?"

"Brother, it was Pondai. That stupid boy cannot keep a secret. Every herd boy knows his chest is too loose."

"Tapera you haven't answered me yet. What did Pondai say?"

"He told them it was in our homestead and it was you who had married a new bride."

"Then what else did they say?"

"Nothing. They thanked him and left in the direction of our well in the stream."

"When did this happen?"

"Just now. When I came here, they were on their way in that direction."

"It's okay Tapera. Thank you for being vigilant. Go back to your herd of animals. We will deal with them."

When Tapera was gone, the three men set for the well in different directions. They knew the entire community, having been born and brought up in it. As usual, they were all armed. No man moved around without wielding a weapon. Even a coward would have one or two weapons with him whenever he moved around. Human life was always at the risk of wild animals or human enemies.

Marujata was no longer a new bride in the Chivi homestead. She now knew her way in the entire homestead and surrounding areas.

One cloudy day, Chezhira woke up with a sore head. She had a fever. In two days, she started developing a bruise on her left thigh, facing the right one. "It is a boil," her mother had said. The following two days were worse. She could neither walk nor eat. Now the bruisy boil was big and reddish on the tip.

Because Chezhira was sick, Marujata now had no companion within the family. Of course, there were other girls who were Runesu's half-sisters, but Marujata was not close to them. Even they slightly distanced themselves from her. That was how life in a polygamous family was. Marujata was aware of that, having been a product of a polygamous family herself. That was why, when she arrived in Chivi's homestead, she quickly chose Chezhira as a companion, because she was born of the same mother as her husband's. "So precious is the mother's breast," elders always said. This proverb meant that whenever favour was to be distributed amongst kinsmen, those born of the same mother chose each other first, then followed those born of the same father, down to the last member of the extended family.

Marujata was done with all chores of the yard. Firewood was plenty in the *bakwa*. Being a basic daily requirement, water supply was always needed. Marujata now knew the way to the well by herself. She told her mother-in-law that she was setting off for the well.

"My child, I don't mean to send you to fetch water alone, but look, your sister-in-law is sick. Had it not been for my aching back, I would have been going with you."

"Don't worry mother. I will be alright. I will be back soon. I now know my way to and from the well."

"Then farewell my good daughter."

"Alright mother." With these words having been said, Marujata set off for the well.

At the well Marujata placed her gourd on an earth pedestal that some unknown woman of the village had created. Now, every woman who came to fetch water at the well used this creation, where every gourd whether big or small sat in comfort.

Marujata was scooping water from the well with her cup made out of the same gourd plant that made gourds for storing water.

Her gourd was almost full when she heard a rustling sound from the nearby bushes. She turned her head to have a thorough check.

All of a sudden, a man came out of the bushes. Marujata jumped from where she was squatting. In a split of a second, a second man followed. She quickly recognised this second man, Mufakose, the man to whom her father had married her off. The two men walked straight to her and stood a few metres away as was the custom. Men and women kept a distance apart from each other. Although Marujata was shocked, she did not run away. She stood there motionless like she had germinated a taproot.

"Hello, beautiful daughter of Makoni. The she-buffalo whose crown shines brighter than gold. The one who does not eat okra. The one who is saluted by those who bring a basket of rice to her. *Hagamukaka,* the metal that sharpens other metals."

It was then that Marujata recognised Jekanyika. Other than being Mufakose's friend, she knew Jekanyika as the village poet. The best poet she had ever known; the poet who entertained villagers at local festivals.

Marujata nearly melted with such words of praise. The way the old man praised her with words meant for people of high status amazed her.

"Hello Makoni's daughter. Hello MaNyati." Mufakose spoke with an unusual voice, as a result of suppressing his anger. A woman was addressed by the name of her people or her totem.

Marujata remained silent. She was out of words. If she had wanted to reply to the salutations, she had to be on her knees as according to the custom. But she found it difficult to kneel down. *What are these men's intentions?*

"You don't remain silent when a man who is your husband is saluting you. In fact, it is supposed to be you greeting us with your knees on the ground. Now to show us your utter rudeness you remain standing up, as if men of this community are now equal to women. Is that so? Has the custom changed? Did your people tell you that women are equal to men?" Mufakose continued like a raging unattended veld fire.

"Please, say something! Are we talking to ourselves? Didn't your elders tell you that if you keep quiet when someone is speaking to you, you are making him or her a fool?"

Still, Marujata kept quiet and frightened. How could she have answered those questions without angering the men?

"*Eee* Makoni's daughter, do you know that for a number of years you were Mufakose's wife? Do you know that your husband Mufakose paid *rovora* to your father? Full *rovora* payment. Whether you answer those questions or not is not my concern. Our people say a word cannot be blocked the way one blocks a fist in a fight. All I know is that those two are ears at both sides of your head, and I know they are in sound condition." This was Jekanyika, still speaking slowly with his poetic voice. He continued.

"We hear you eloped to another man with your father still in possession of Mufakose's wealth. How do you expect that knot to be untied?"

The three were locked in conversation, so they did not notice the arrival of Runesu and his friends. They saw them when they were close by. The three men came close and made a half circle around the well. Marujata was still at her spot.

She was almost inside the half circle. Jekanyika and Mufakose moved backwards, leaving a respectable distance apart.

Toindepi was at one end of the half circle close to Jekanyika. His shining, well-sharpened spear was up with its stabbing end pointing skywards. His bare chest revealed his muscles which he took pride in contracting and expanding.

Gwenzi was on the other end of the half circle towards Mufakose. He too had his chest out, a sign of a man proud of his masculinity.

Runesu was in the middle of the half circle twisting his neck from right to left, then from left to right like a wrestler who is about to step into a fighting arena.

No man spoke. No one greeted the other. Only eyes and bodies moved as if it was a group of deaf men having a meeting. All five men stood still, staring at one another with eyes that spoke an unknown language.

"MaNyati." Toindepi broke the silence. Marujata looked up at the mention of her maiden name.

"Is your gourd full?"

"It is half-way full." Marujata was bold enough to answer amid shivers.

"Fill it up then."

Marujata stared around the men with her eyes moving from men to men.

"Fill it up MaNyati." Toindepi ordered.

Marujata walked to the well where she was squatting before when Mufakose and Jekanyika arrived. She took her cup and filled her gourd. All men had their eyes fixed on her, like men looking at worms coming out of meat they were about to roast.

When the gourd was full Toindepi spoke again.

"Carry it now and head home." Upon Toindepi's command Marujata lifted the gourd and laid it on her head with all men's eyes transfixed on her.

"Move on MaNyati. Runesu, follow behind her."

Mufakose and Jekanyika knew they could not match these young men, but they had to say something.

"Men of Gokuda, what do you really intend to do?" Mufakose asked with a low voice.

"It's us who should be asking you this question. This well belongs to villagers of the western end, so what has brought you here all the way from the eastern end?"

"You speak like you are a foreigner here. Who doesn't know that Makoni's daughter is my wife? I paid her *rovora* in full. Does that not make her my wife, in accordance with our custom?"

"Thank you old man for being well versed in matters of our people, but don't speak as if Makoni's daughter is an animal. She is human and adult enough to do what she chooses. Did you propose love to her? It's true that you paid *rovora* to her father, but if you didn't propose love, then you jumped protocols. You should have won her heart first. How did you old men, her father and you sit to discuss a marriage custom for someone without her consent?"

"That's why I said you speak like a foreigner young man. Is this custom new here? Am I the one who started it?"

"We don't care which male chauvinist started it!"

"Male chauvinist! Really? Who is more chauvinist than the other, a man who force-marches a woman to his people and a man who pays *rovora* for the same woman?"

"Old man, we cannot spend the whole day arguing with each other like women, you know very well to whom you gave your wealth. Go and confront him for reimbursement. We are done with you." Toindepi concluded as the four of them left the stream in a single file. Mufakose and Jekanyika were left rooted at their spots with no words to say.

Chapter 8

Tanaka was the eldest of Makoni's sons, born from the same womb as Marujata. Marujata was the eldest daughter. During her absence, Sekai, her half-sister, had taken her place in all feminine chores of the homestead.

One day, Tanaka and his young brother Zvidzai were going to a nearby forest to cut a big log from a marula tree trunk. With the log, Tanaka wanted to carve a mortar for his mother. Her old one had recently developed a crack.

"Your sisters always leave it in the sun and sometimes in the rain, no wonder why it's like this. The weather affected it. If only you could make a new one, my son." His mother had sadly told him. It was because of his empathy for his mother that he had wholeheartedly obeyed. He had accepted the request just like any other son would have done to his beloved mother.

As the two young men were just a few yards from the family yard, they met Punha who was coming from the opposite direction. The girl gave way for the boys by moving off the footpath, as was the custom when female members of the community met male members. Yes, they would keep a distance apart.

"Good afternoon boys."

"Good afternoon Punha."

"Is Sekai home?"

"Ooh yes. We left her grinding peanut butter." Tanaka answered, not really minding her.

"It's okay. Allow me to see her then."

"It's alright."

Punha spoke as if she wanted permission from the boys to see their sister. She passed by. After walking a few yards, she looked back at the boys. She continued walking again for a while, stopped and looked back again. This time her eyes came in contact with Zvidzai's.

"Brother did you see how that girl Punha looked at you?"

"No l didn't."

"Ummmm those were talking eyes I tell you."

"Talking about what, Zvidzai?" Tanaka chuckled.

"This is not the first time I saw her looking at you like that. Even Sekai knows that a day never passes without her mentioning your name. That girl has a crush on you I tell you."

"Zvidzai your brains are too speedy. Is it possible for a girl to propose love to a man?"

"Not that she will propose, maybe she is waiting for you to propose." Zvidzai tittered.

"Zvidzai, don't make me laugh. Punha is not beautiful. I don't love her. A girl with cracks on her feet like Punha must get a man from far away villages not here in Tseisi village. Do you know what I heard? She wets her blankets in her sleep?"

"*Eee* brother, tell me you are joking. Wetting her blankets at that age?"

"Yes. She is not wife material." The brothers laughed as they walked towards the forest.

Punha lived several homesteads from Makoni's, in the same village of Tseisi. Her father was one of the spirit mediums of the community. He also doubled as the community *nyusa*, rainmaker. He was the announcer of the *mutoro*, beer brewed to appease the gods of rains. These gods brought adequate rains so that the community could have bumper harvests. The ceremony of *mutoro* was held towards the rain season, at the end of the spring season. Each villager was made to bring a portion of rapoko or millet for beer brewing. The beer was brewed by the oldest women who were past childbearing age. If they needed assistance with minor things, little girls who had not yet reached puberty were always at their disposal.

Punha had no known boyfriend in the entire village of Tseisi and beyond. Some villagers attributed her failure to be courted to her father's high status, with some disputing that concept. Yes, Hoko her father was a respected man in the whole community. Headmen, the chief, messengers and commoners all revered him. No man would dare disrespect a man who was the spirits' mouth. He was considered one of the wisest men in the Mposi community. Before any man knew what laid ahead of their lives, Hoko would have foreseen and foretold it. Headmen and chiefs consulted him whenever they had a riddle that needed his divine scrutiny.

Hoko was probably the only man with a single wife. The spirits did not allow his medium to marry multiple wives, because they would disturb his job with their numerous demands. Other spirits preferred single men as mediums, the villagers said.

Tanaka and Zvidzai did not take long in the forest. They returned with the marula log and began carving the mortar whilst seated in the shade of a *musasa* tree on the outskirts of their yard. Chenai, their little sister brought them a gourd of *maheu* and they took turns sipping the sour drink.

"Brother, you see when it's hot like this, that drink made from marula fruits would have done us better." Zvidzai was a talkative guy. A fly could not settle on his lips, everybody said.

"Ooh you mean *mukumbi*? Yaa that drink is excellent, but when you are at work like this you don't drink too much of it, lest you get intoxicated."

"People at work drink fresh *mukumbi*. That fermented one is too strong."

"Yes, especially the one Mai Simba brews; it's terrible. Hardly do people who drink her *mukumbi* depart her place without having a fight. You remember a week before last week, Gumhai the Chief's messenger fought with Bopoto after having too much of her drink."

"Zvidzai, I don't drink Mai Simba's *mukumbi*."

"Why brother?" Zvidzai looked surprised.

"Ummmm Zvidzai, you are still a toddler with mother's milk on your nose. Didn't you hear that Mai Simba is a witch?" Tanaka whispered. A rumour, if heard by someone who did not keep secrets was dangerous. The person alleged to have said it could be arraigned before the headman's court for trial. Every villager dreaded going to the courts because few people would succeed in convincing the court that they were innocent.

"Brother, you mean you believe Bopoto that nuisance who beat his mother and ended up performing a *kutanda botso* ritual?"

"Zvidzai, many people are saying so. The entire community says so. It's only that Bopoto does not know how to keep a secret. Even if a secret is harmless when said, you don't have to trust him. He does not mind the implications of his utterances. But see, elders say where there is smoke there is bound to be fire. And again, this rumour did not start now. It's an old rumour that I grew up hearing since I was a toddler. I heard about her witchcraft before Bopoto's nonsensical speeches." Tanaka was still whispering.

"So, brother tell me? Why had father married off sister Marujata to Mufakose? Didn't he know that his senior wife walks naked during the night? Didn't he know that his senior wife exhumes the dead out of their graves for flesh consumption?"

"Every villager was wondering. This is why mother didn't want Mufakose to marry off sister Maru." Marujata was also called Maru by her kinsmen, an abbreviation of her name.

"So, you mean with her now married to Runesu, mother is happy?" Zvidzai asked with keen interest.

"I can say yes. Why? Because one day I overheard her saying that Runesu was better because he is single and also of the same age as sister Maru. In terms of wealth, both families are rich."

"But will father bless that marriage?"

"Zvidzai, the problem with our father is that he married off sister Maru some years ago. Mufakose gave him all the wealth that he demanded as *rovora*. Now he has since squandered all the wealth. Under normal circumstances, father is supposed to give back Mufakose his wealth and a token of fine for time wasted and breach of contract. As it is my brother, where do you think our father can get the wealth to pay back Mufakose, for I don't see sister Maru coming back? Even so, what man can take back a woman who has been made a wife by another man for close to four moons now? The Chivis have already incorporated our sister in their family as their daughter-in-law. She has been presented before their gods as per custom. How do we take her back?"

"I think mother is right. Let sister Maru marry Runesu. He is better than Mufakose, as long as he keeps our sister happy. But who will be bold enough to confront father without receiving some beating?"

"Father does not consult anyone. Neither does he listen to advice. If he was a good listener of advice, he would have been one of the richest men in Tseisi village, but alas he squandered everything that his father left for him. We wouldn't be suffering with the vast wealth that our grandfather had."

The mortar was beginning to shape up. Now Tanaka was chipping out the hole that was to accommodate grains for pounding. His intentions were to finish the carving that day and do the final touches the following day.

That evening Makoni came home early for the first time in years. He brought home a guinea fowl. He wanted Gambiza to make the best meal for the family.

"But Master it's not enough. You know how big this family is." Gambiza reminded him. Makoni frowned before saying anything.

"That bird is for adults. You and me. So, you mean it's not enough for two people?"

"What about the children?"

"Which children? Do you think I can hunt and bring home meat for Tanaka and his brothers? They are men enough and should be providing for the family."

"What about girls? Should they go hunting also?"

"Woman, you talk too much. Which girls? Sekai and her sisters should have found men to marry them. Look, Marujata is gone, isn't it they are almost of the same age? Your problem is that you hide this fact from these girls. Tell them straight to their faces that a girl child belongs to her husband's people, not here. Here she is a passer-by. How do you keep a girl child at home for donkey years as if she is haunted by the spirits of spinsters?"

"Master, you are diverting from my point. My point is we cannot eat meat while children have vegetables."

"Then give them soup."

"No, I won't do that. I will slaughter one of my cocks."

"Be it the way you deem necessary but let me give you a piece of advice. You are spoiling your children. They shall humiliate you one day before visitors." Gambiza did not reply. She walked away and mumbled, "I have never seen a man of the buffalo totem who is very greedy like this. Meat greed is associated with those of the lion totem." She had thought Makoni was far away to hear her. But he heard her.

"And those of Moyo totem are not greedy, eh? You forget that your father Sinyoro, when he was alive, nearly killed a stranger who tempered with his snare."

"Makoni stop it! Don't you know it's sacred to speak bad about a deceased man?" This time she did not address him as Master, as was the custom when a married woman addressed her husband. Makoni knew she was angry and kept quiet as open acceptance of wrongdoing.

Hours later in the evening Makoni was seated on his inclining wooden stool, smoking his pipe. The aroma of roasted meat and burnt millet-meal from his wife's kitchen made his mouth watery. After a while Svodai, one of his daughters brought him food.

"Svodai, how many times should I tell you to kneel down when giving adults something?" Gambiza shouted from the inside of the kitchen. Svodai folded one knee and quickly stood up in what they called *kutyora muzura,* a curtsy. This salutation was done by women who met adults on their way, for they could not kneel on the ground when passing by.

"Both your knees must touch the ground!" Gambiza emphasised, to which the poor girl obeyed.

"It's your fault if she is morally loose. You will be embarrassed when she is accused of misbehaviour by her man's people, for they will say her mother and aunts did not do enough to educate her." Gambiza did not reply, albeit she knew what Makoni said was true.

That night they had a decent meal, something Makoni's children had longed for. Even toddlers could be heard laughing and teasing each other. Others were throwing bones to one another with soup-smeared hands. "Everyone wants a good life," so goes the Karanga proverb.

After eating, Makoni went into his hut and retired to bed. Older boys also went to their hut. Older girls made the cooking hut tidy before leaving for their rooms. Svodai was sent to fetch firewood at the family *bakwa*. Those who used the cooking hut as their sleeping room needed fire. She came back running faster than she went.

"What is it you timid girl? You frighten us!"

"There it is! There outside by the *bakwa*." The little girl stammered. Gambiza and the other girls and little boys were shocked. Gambiza peered through a space on the doorway. Sure, a human-looking figure was at the outskirts of the yard. It looked like it was in a kneeling position.

"You remain here all of you." Gambiza said to her kids. She tiptoed to their sleeping room and called her husband.

"Let's hope you are not disturbing my sleep for nothing." Makoni took his knobkerrie and came out of the hut barefooted. They both walked towards the alleged figure.

"Who are you?" Makoni barked. The figure remained motionless and speechless.

"I said who are you? Speak before I crush your head into sap, speak!"

The figure coughed what sounded like a sigh. It fidgeted slightly. Both pairs of eyes were on it.

"I am Tanaka."

"Tanaka?"

"Tanaka who?"

"Tanaka Makoni." Both adults sighed. Gambiza carried both her hands on her head in utter amazement.

Chapter 9

The following day, Makoni sent his son Matenda to call his relatives for a family meeting. He wanted all his kinsmen to gather at his place. If a man who behaves like a madman whenever drunk is deprived of that which makes him intoxicated and sobriety visits him, he becomes a sane man. Such was the situation with Makoni. His senses were in a state of wellness.

His kinsmen started flocking in, one by one. Each made a shout of salutation as they arrived in their kin's homestead. Makoni's little boys brought stools for everyone. In a short while, everyone was seated awaiting Makoni's address.

"Excuse me my kinsmen. It's me who called you for a family meeting. I know some of you were busy with your jobs, but you saw it good to come here. I thank you. Elders say when a kinsman's beard is on fire, you come and extinguish it without delay. My cousins, your kinsman is burning. Yes, burning like hell." Makoni paused and gazed at the circle of his kinsmen seated.

"We are all ears, go ahead." One of them said with a voice that seemed at ease.

"Double trouble is when a mother burns her back and her child burns its belly. This is the situation I am in."

"Makoni, will you please stop beating about the bush. Get to the point." Another elderly of his kinsmen said.

"I am talking to adults. Riddles are a communication mode of our people. Is there anyone who doesn't understand my speech? For this is not Buja, Tavara or *Putukezi* language."

"It's alright, go ahead, because if we start arguing now, we end up finding it difficult to make head or tail of the whole discussion. Proceed." Another elderly who was the eldest of all Makoni men ordered.

"I have two situations that need your assistance. Initially I wanted to call you for this first one when a recent one occurred last night." Makoni paused again and examined his audience's attention. All men were quiet, so he continued.

"I think you all know that some years ago I married off my daughter Marujata to Mufakose. That man paid everything we agreed on as you all know. Now this son of Chivi took away my daughter and made her his wife knowing full well that she is somebody's wife. This is not allowed. According to our people's ways of living you know it's a crime. This has given me a headache. Chivi sent a messenger here on two occasions. I set my sons and dogs on each messenger sent. Now it's close to four months since Marujata became their bride, which means she is no longer a pure woman. You know what I mean. Again, our culture does not allow us to retrieve a daughter who has been sexually tempered with by a man. Who do you think can remarry her? Her dignity has already been tarnished. So, my people what should I do?"

After a while, up stood Zenda whose father was brother to Makoni's father.

"Your case which involves another family does not need our family to preside over. Our hands are tied. Kinsmen solve issues that are confined within the family structures. My opinion is that you need to see the headman and explain your case."

"And what will our headman do, considering that Chivi is not of this village? Chivi is from Gokuda and we are from here in Tseisi village."

Each man spoke how he viewed the case.

"Such cases are not new amongst our people. We have seen many of such cases before, where a man from one village offends a man in the other village. Yes, you inform our headman. He is the head of this village..."

"Fine but can he subpoena a man who is not under his jurisdiction to his court?"

"Order my people. Let's behave ourselves." Nearly everyone wanted to say something but Zenda calmed the situation to silence.

60

"You cut me short. Yes, Chivi is not under Tseisi's jurisdiction, so what must be done? It's according to the laws of this empire that you inform your headman. Your headman in turn informs Gokuda as headman to Chivi. Gokuda in turn arraigns his subject Chivi to his court. But the case has to be tried in the Chief's court because no headman has the power to subpoena another headman, because their powers are equal. That is how I saw such cases being solved by our fathers and grandfathers."

"So, you mean we just inform the headman, and the rest is his part to play?"

"Sure. Sure, that's it." Everybody agreed with Zenda and the matter was laid to rest.

"Now comes this one which happened yesterday. Last night I had retired to bed when Gambiza woke me up to tell me that there was a human-like figure in a kneeling position at the outskirts of the yard. They said Svodai, my daughter, spotted it first."

Everybody was paying attention like a family listening to a diviner's revelations. Makoni continued uninterrupted.

"I had wondered what spirit could visit me at that juncture, for I have offended no spirit. I haven't transgressed the laws of our ancestors, so I confronted the figure with the courage of a lioness protecting its cubs. I ordered the figure to speak out. It was a female figure. Hoko's daughter. I asked who she was. She said she was Tanaka. I said Tanaka who. She said Tanaka Makoni. My people, when someone's daughter comes into your homestead in such fashion and you ask her who she is, when she mentions one of your son's names, you know what it means culturally." When Makoni finished his speech, every man made a sigh of relief.

"Did you ask our son whose name was mentioned about it?"

"Yes, I did, but he alleged ignorance of the lady's claim."

"Do you know the girl? I mean Hoko's daughter?"

"I didn't until Gambiza told me she is a friend to my daughter Sekai."

"And you asked Sekai if she knew anything about the two's relationship?"

Questions rained on Makoni like a hailstorm.

"Sekai said the two are not in any relationship, unless she was siding with her brother."

"Is the girl here?"

"Yes, she is here. Where should I have chased her to, worse when she had mentioned my son's name?"

"Call her. I have a few questions to ask her for the sake of clarity."

Makoni called one of his youngest daughters.

"Call your mother for me."

In a short time Gambiza came and knelt a respectful distance from the men.

"You sent for me Master."

"Yes, my dear wife. Call your new daughter-in-law for me. We need her here. Also bring with you your son Tanaka."

Makoni was a man who would hide all his bad behaviour when they had visitors. One would have thought he was a loving and caring husband when he addressed his wife by saying 'my dear wife'

Punha came accompanied by Gambiza. Tanaka followed from a distance behind. They both knelt where Gambiza had knelt before. Tanaka found his own spot and sat down. According to Karanga culture adults did not greet younger members first, but it was the young ones who greeted adults first. Punha greeted them and quickly resorted to silent mode. Tanaka had greeted them when they arrived.

He only said, "*Pachipamwe.*" This was a salutation done by someone who would have greeted you before.

"*Pamweni.*" They all chorused in reply.

"I heard that you are the daughter of Hoko. Is that so?" Zenda asked.

"Yes." Punha answered with her head bowed down and slightly tilted to the left, a sign of pleading for pity.

"We heard your story. Can I ask you something, daughter of Hoko?" Punha nodded.

"Are you two in a relationship?" Zenda's pointing finger moved from Punha to Tanaka and back again to Punha. Punha hesitated.

"Let me first ask you, young lady. Are you in a relationship with him?"

Punha took a while to answer.

"No."

"Did I hear well? Did she say they are not in a relationship?" Zenda searched the entire circle of men for a confirmation.

"Yes, we heard her well. She said they are not!" The elders shouted.

"But you came here last night and when asked who you are, you mentioned his name. Do you know what that means culturally?"

"Yes." Punha answered in a barely audible whisper.

"So, you mean you want this boy to marry you?"

"Yes." Punha was bold enough to answer.

"Alright you can all leave."

Gambiza and Punha rose up and walked away. Tanaka followed in a different direction.

The gathering of elders had a small talk after which Tanaka was called back. Zenda, who was always the most talkative, maybe because they respected his age, proceeded.

"My son, of all men of Tseisi I am one of the few who saw the sun earlier than the rest." The old man bragged with the voice of authority. He sounded like a god addressing humans.

"Our people have a marriage custom called *kuganha,* where a lady elopes to a boy whom she loves despite the fact that the boy has not proposed love to her. It is a sign that she has no option, because she cannot force the boy to propose love to her. This is what Hoko's daughter did to you last night. By virtue of what she did, and according to our culture, the Karanga people, she is now your wife. A lady who does a *kuganha* custom is not chased away. Now, having spent a night here it's worse. Her people cannot allow her back. They assume she has been made a wife during the night. This is how our culture is." All eyes were on Tanaka who was speechless, anxiety taking a toll on his system.

The gathering had dispersed when Tanaka sat down under the shade of the *musasa* tree where he was carving a mortar the previous day. He tried to finish off the mortar, but it was a fact that he was bodily there but mentally absent. What elder Zenda told him about their custom was not new to him. He grew up hearing explanations of such a custom, but still he had no feelings for Punha. *Why did she choose me, of all the boys of this village? That girl must be mad. How can a boy from a poor family like mine marry a daughter of the most respected man in this community? What will her father say when he hears that his daughter eloped to Makoni's homestead? This girl has thrown pepper into my eyes. Hey, it's tough. It's worrisome*, Tanaka thought to himself.

Chapter 10

Chief Mposi's palace was situated on a high hill overlooking the river Mwenezi. Standing on this site, one would have a full view of the community he presided over, except a few features that were too far away or partially obstructed.

Several huts stood scattered haphazardly like mushrooms within the palace grounds. Many of those huts belonged to his eighteen wives. Ooh yes, if every man in that community had more than one wife, it was understandable that a chief had such numerous wives. He had many children too. During his younger years, he knew how many children he had, but later on he lost count as they increased by five or six every passing year. Chief Mposi's palace was more like a vast complex than a mere homestead.

Makoni had done exactly what was agreed upon by his kinsmen at the family meeting. He had visited Headman Tseisi and narrated his story. The headman promised to send a messenger to Headman Gokuda. When Headman Gokuda had heard what Headman Tseisi's messenger had said, he sent his own messenger to summon Chivi. Chivi was supposed to bring all his family members involved in the court case for interrogation. After that, both headmen agreed to inform the Chief of the verdict. A date for the court was set by the chief.

Chivi brought along his son Runesu and his friends. His senior wife who happened to be Runesu's mother, Marujata, his now daughter-in-law and other members of his family who had volunteered were also in attendance.

Makoni brought along his wife, mother to Marujata, his sisters and a few members of his family, whereas Mufakose's entourage was composed of men only. All were his kinsmen except for his friend Jekanyika. All groups brought a goat each, in case it was demanded by the chief. Gumhai, the chief's messenger, ushered them to the courtyard. They all sat in a half-circle before the chief's throne. The chief was not there.

Chief Mposi was a stout man with a massive belly that made him walk with much difficulty. He came flanked by his two guards. A crown of royalty made of pure gold sat on his head and a leopard skin draped over his right shoulder, beneath a huge necklace made of crocodile teeth. In his hand was a small elephant tusk. His bottom was covered by the skins of a lion. On his throne were all sorts of decorations; different minerals that glittered to onlookers and hides of special animals. Lion and leopard hides were only used by chiefs. No ordinary man was allowed to wear them, even if they were the ones who had killed the animals. If by chance a man killed such an animal, he was to bring the hide to the chief without waiting for the chief's request, because it was deemed common knowledge that such precious items were reserved for chiefs and other respected traditional leaders.

When the chief and his entourage reached his throne, everybody stood up as a sign of loyalty. He stood for a while facing the group of people before him. They all chorused,

"*Changamire!*" Women knelt and clapped their hands while men bowed their heads as a sign of respect.

After a while, Taruvinga, one of the chief's advisors, rose up and said, "Excuse me Your Highness Chief Mposi. *Mhukahuru*, the Big Animal. The one who rules the wise. The stupid, he discards. The one who sits on hot porridge with buttocks that don't burn. The fearless and most feared."

Everybody roared, "*Changamire!*"

The chief nodded in approval. He felt honoured by his subjects, with such words of praise.

Taruvinga continued. "Excuse me all chief's advisors, messengers, headmen and all parents who are gathered in this courtyard."

The advisor paused and stared at the crowd to confirm their attention. Sure, all of them were attentive.

"Chief, today we have a case of marriage wrangle between three families. Two of them are from Gokuda village. I think Gokuda is here. The other family is from Tseisi village. I can see Tseisi over there. Allow me to call upon Makoni to stand up and narrate his story. Stand up Makoni!"

Makoni did not waste any time. From the day he had brought home a guinea fowl, he had not taken any beer in his mouth. He was as sober as a sane man. "For there is a thin line between drunkenness and madness," Tseisi used to tell his people back in his village. Makoni was asked to make a payment of a goat to the court. The goat was slaughtered, and meat roasted for all palace workers that helped in court trials and prosecutions.

"Honourable Chief. Honourable Advisors, messengers and all villagers gathered here. My name is Makoni of Tseisi village. I think all of you know me."

Almost all villagers nodded their heads in confirmation.

"Makoni is your clan name. You are not your forefather." The Chief interrupted.

"Yes, Your Highness. My name is Tadzembga Makoni. Since my father's death, people have known me as Makoni, our clan name."

"Go ahead, we know your clan from your forefathers who migrated from the east in the land of the Manyika."

"Sure, Your Highness. My case is as follows. Some years ago, I married off my daughter who is over there to Mufakose of Gokuda village. He paid all *rovora* instalments. But because my daughter was too young, we agreed that Mufakose would take her to his homestead when she was old enough to be of wife use. This was done on a mutual contract.

Now the problem that made me seek justice from your court, Changamire, is that four months ago my daughter went missing. We searched for her to no avail, until a *munyai* sent by Chivi came to my place to try to enter into marriage talks with me. My sons chased him away. He sent a second *munyai*. I chased him away too. My question is, how can a man deliberately marry someone's wife? This is my case, Your Highness." Makoni sat down after finishing his speech.

Taruvinga came forward and said:

"Your Highness. *Mhukahuru*, this is Makoni's narrative."

Chief Mposi stared at the crowd before him and coughed boastfully and said, "Can the said girl stand up please?"

"Young woman, stand up!" Taruvinga commanded. Marujata rose up from amongst the crowd of women and stood with her head slightly bowed as a sign of both respect and shyness.

"Old women of this community, can you examine that girl with your eyes and tell me something?" The rest of the crowd stared at the group of women. All eyes of the women were transfixed on Marujata.

"Did anyone see something?" One woman stood up to answer.

"Yes woman, speak." Taruvinga gave her an opportunity to speak.

"She looks like she had skipped her moon."

"Thank you, woman. You can sit down." The chief said in a low tone.

"My people, most cases that you bring here are a result of you abusing our culture. Our fathers left us a pure culture, intact with all customary laws, but you have abused them.

First of all, who doesn't know that if a man marries off his daughter, the new son-in-law takes his wife soon after paying all agreed *rovora* instalments? How was it possible for Makoni to keep his daughter for such a number of years without him handing her over to her husband? And you Mufakose, how did you patiently spend those years after full *rovora* without claiming your wife? Do you see where you people made it difficult for yourselves? When our elders made this law, that a girl married off to a man must immediately start to live in her husband's homestead, no matter how young she is. They knew such circumstances were bound to happen. Now look, the girl is pregnant by another man. How are you going to reverse that? Chivi, do you see this is a difficult knot to untie?" Chivi stood up and saluted the chief and his advisors.

"Honourable Chief these are mischievous behaviours of children. Our elders say, a man who begets a son brings trouble in his homestead. When you sire a child you sire flesh, but not his spirit. We do try and teach them our people's culture, but it seems our words enter with this ear and come out through the other ear. I hereby accept all offences levelled against me, because if my son is guilty am I left innocent? Yes, I am guilty as well."

"Chivi, will you stop your cheap proverbial rants! Do you realise that being residents of the same village, you and Mufakose, it's obvious your son knew that girl was married off to Mufakose."?

"Sure, Your Highness."

"What is sure? That you accept guilt here before my court? Why didn't you accept guilt to Mufakose and save time? *Hee*?" The chief roared, mad with anger like a male buffalo injured by a hunter's arrow.

"Your Highness, our elders say an offence is not committed by a log, but it is committed by a human being. If a god can be appeased, why not a man whose offender accepts wrong-doing?"

"Chivi you speak defensively, as if your son did it willingly. Your speech shows no remorse. A man who wants peace in his entire life must start the journey by respecting his kinsmen, neighbours, other villagers and strangers, above all the spirits of this land. Sit down! Taruvinga, allow Mufakose to stand up." The chief fidgeted in his seat and inclined back as he usually did on all court days. "Mufakose you can stand up."

Mufakose rose up from where he was seated, bowed his head and said:

"Changamire. Allow your dog to bark."

"Let it bark." The chief replied authoritatively. His voice carried a tone of command.

"As you all heard, this is the story. I accept where both of us, my in-law Makoni and I made a mistake that Chivi's son capitalised on. But a man who takes someone's wife knowingly belittles him and his manhood. He is saying I am not man enough. In simple terms, he is saying I am a woman. That kind of provocation, *Mhukahuru*, is not good for the peace of this land. Of course, today I may accept being paid back what I am owed, but no amount of wealth will erase my tarnished dignity, and for that I do not have space in my heart to accommodate his apology."

Chief Mposi was a wise man endowed with Solomonic wisdom. As Mufakose spoke, he was listening to every word said.

"So, you mean even after being given back your wealth you still feel it's not enough appeasement?"

"Sure, Your Highness."

"Did you hear him carefully? I reckon all of you are adults. You understand the language of our people whether one speaks in proverbs, idioms or figurative expressions. Mark his words so that when something tragic between his family and that of Chivi happens, we will be seated here again trying to equate his words to the events that would have happened."

Mufakose knew what the chief meant, but because of anger, he did not retract his speech.

"It's okay Mufakose you can sit down. Let's proceed. Makoni, how are you going to pay back Mufakose? Do you have his wealth?"

"No. I don't have it, *Mhukahuru*."

"You don't have it? You squandered what your son-in-law paid when you knew very well you were in possession of your daughter? *Hee*? The same daughter Mufakose gave you wealth for? Taruvinga, can you explain again to the court how our people deal with such twisted marriage customs."

"*Mhukahuru* and the entire audience. Our people say there are two ways to end this case. Either Makoni gives Mufakose another of his daughters as replacement for the one who eloped to another man's place, or Makoni pays Mufakose his wealth with a fine of two heads of cattle on top. If the father-in-law, in this case Makoni, does not have the wealth with which to pay back, then his new son-in-law who snatched his daughter from her rightful husband must pay *rovora* in full, then with that wealth the father-in-law gives it to his offended old son-in-law. This way, the case is solved. Chief, have I made it clear?"

"You nailed it home to listeners who have ears, Taruvinga. The good part of ears is that they are not like mouths and eyes, they are ever open. So, no-one can wake up tomorrow and say I did not hear him saying so, unless one is absent."

Silence swept across the courtyard as if a goddess of war had passed through the area.

"I think you all heard what Taruvinga said. Chivi, give *rovora* to Makoni. Makoni, when the *rovora* instalments are settled, give back Mufakose his wealth together with a fine of two heads of cattle. Then bring one head of cattle here as the court fine. The court proceeding ends now. Go well. Please live peacefully. No more quarrels. We are not quarrelsome people, right?" Everybody nodded except for Mufakose.

Chapter 11

A week had passed with Punha in Makoni's homestead. She was adapting to life as a daughter-in-law, but she had not seen Tanaka face to face. Both of them dreaded the day they would meet. Were it not for Chief Mposi's court that tried Marujata's case, the marriage rite between Tanaka and Punha would have been done by then.

Tanaka had no feelings for Punha. He had actually despised her publicly, but Punha was not a girl that would easily give up. She was constructive in her persuasion, particularly when she knew odds were stacked against her.

"Love hurts like a thorn in the flesh." A distant friend had asked her why she loved a boy who seemed not to care about her, a boy from a poor family for that matter. "Our people have several different marriage customs. The rich can confront the family of a girl they intend to marry, for marriage contracts. Some girls elope to their men. Some boys snatch their girlfriends without their would-be in-laws' knowledge. Some men are given wives of their deceased brothers. Still, other girls are married off by their parents. Whereas the poor men work for their wives. All of them are our people's ways of marriage." Punha had explained. She saw no exception in her marriage. It was just as good as any other.

Makoni's homestead had constant issues that needed his undivided attention. He had promised his wife that he wanted to be a changed man. If a man sees his household in tatters due to his own undoing, then transformation was his best way out. Six days had passed without him taking any strong drink, except for two cups of *mukumbi*, the marula drink that Taruvona brought for him. "The two cups are enough for me," Makoni had openly told Taruvona. He had shown him a cold shoulder, only that Taruvona was stupid. An adult who is sane must realise where he is not welcome.

Makoni now wanted to associate with people of better status in the village, people who could impart something meaningful to his life.

"Master!"

"Yes Gambiza."

"Will you come sit here please, I want to have a talk with you."

"It is a man who has diarrhoea who pulls the door open. It is also one who is cold who pulls the blanket. Isn't it?"

"Alright then, let me take my mat and come there."

"Sure."

Gambiza left whatever she was doing and headed to where Makoni was seated. She unfolded her mat and sat with both legs spread apart. She stared at her husband straight in his face, as if she was seeing him for the first time.

"What is it again? Will I ever know peace in this land?"

"When the gods give you a wound, they mean flies must feed on you."

"Go ahead. A man's ears are always open when his wife opens her mouth to say a speech of sense, but they automatically shut down for nonsensical statements."

"It's a harmless speech of sense."

"Alright, speak Gambiza daughter of Sinyoro."

"*Eee* Master, it's been long since this daughter of Hoko has been here. We haven't given her to her husband."

"Ooh I was thinking about it. Nothing can stop us now. We can do it tonight."

"But Tanaka seems to dislike the lady."

"Gambiza, you know our culture very well. Even your son Tanaka is aware of it. No man refuses a woman who elopes into his family for marriage. Let us not tire from teaching our children the ways of our people, lest we bring up a mischievous generation that will offend our ancestors and they, in turn will remove their protection from us."

"Yes, he is aware of our culture."

"We don't know what that daughter of Hoko saw in him that attracted her. If you put a heifer and a lazy bull in the

73

same kraal they will eventually produce a calf, regardless of the bull's laziness."

"Then comes the issue of *rovora*. We cannot keep Hoko's daughter here for a long time without finding common ground with her people. What if she suddenly falls sick or something calamitous happens to her? How will we be able to inform her people?"

"Are you wishing her bad?"

"No. Why would I wish my first daughter-in-law bad?" Silence followed, allowing both adults to grind their thoughts to smoothness.

"Hmmm it's tough, Gambiza. You are aware of our poverty, just like you know the insides of your palm."

"He better take my goats and give his in-laws."

"Who?"

"Who else are we talking about, besides our son Tanaka?"

"Gambiza, do you want to bring evil omen into my family? Where in this land have you seen a mother paying *rovora* for her son? Tanaka is of buffalo totem and you are Sinyoro the heart, so the two of you are not kins. You want to give your son your wealth then when you die your spirit comes to haunt the entire family, saying you took the wealth of a non-relative without compensation? No Gambiza, I say no. Poverty is painful, but it does not kill."

Before supper that evening, Gambiza showed Punha her husband's hut. She started by cleaning it from the walls to the floor. She collected cow dung from the cattle kraal and smeared it on the floor. There were a few things in the house. A reed bed and Tanaka's weapons. Punha got some few materials from Gambiza with which she decorated the interior of the hut. The bedding was white in accordance with custom.

After supper, Tanaka hesitated to enter the hut. He spent some hours in the boys' hut cracking jokes with them. It was almost midnight when he left for his hut. He opened the door without knocking. Punha was seated on the bed sewing something with beans.

"Do you want to kill your eyes? Don't you know sewing at night affects one's sight?"

Tanaka spoke first.

"No, don't worry I will manage. The eye of a bead is bigger than that of a needle."

"Why are you awake at this time, it's almost midnight?"

"But you are also awake. We are both awake aren't we?"

Tanaka kept quiet.

"I was waiting for you. How can I sleep when today is my best day?"

"Ooh best day? Really?"

"Yes. For the past five years I have been stalking you like a hunter after game. But you didn't..."

"Are you crazy? Where have you seen a woman proposing love from a man?"

"I am not proposing anything. We are already husband and wife."

"Punha, do you realise what you have put me into? Your father is a traditional leader. The most respected man of this community. And I am a poor man with nothing to give to a father-in-law. Can you balance that?"

"We approach each problem as it comes. As of now let's solve this."

She rose up from where she was seated and came before Tanaka who was on a stool. She went behind his back and started running her palms on his shoulder. Tanaka felt a sudden sensation running down his spine.

"It is not a woman who should initiate love in your bedroom. Show authority by doing it first." These words were said by their leader at the circumcision ceremony. The event was used as a school where youths were initiated into adulthood.

With this voice resounding in his head, he gathered courage. He did not want Punha to call him a weak and intolerant man. Neither did he want his people to say he was afraid of women.

He stood up and hugged Punha with his huge arms, smooched her at the back and drew her as close to him as possible, her breasts resting on his bare chest. Silence swept across the room with only their heart beats and breaths singing songs of love. Now Punha was dizzy like a drug addict. Tanaka lifted her and laid her on the bed. One thing led to another, until both of them were enveloped in a world of their own where he was the king and she was the queen.

Under normal circumstances, the Makonis should have organised a ceremony for the new bride, but there were no adequate resources to foot the event. Culturally, such events were postponed if the family was not prepared but were never skipped forever. You don't invoke the spirits to welcome a new bride when the bride has not been celebrated. It was considered taboo.

Punha woke up the earliest of them all and started her bridal chores. Other members of the family trickled out of their huts later. Almost all eyes were on Punha who went about with a limp of one trying to suppress agony. Other members of the extended family started flocking in. One of the eldest women went into Tanaka's hut. He had left for the river for fishing with his brothers.

The old woman went straight to the bed, examined the white cloth with curious eyes. There was a small red dot on the cloth. A red spot on a white background is easily noticed even by a short-sighted person.

She went with the folded cloth to a hut where all women gathered. She entered and unfolded the cloth for everyone present to see.

"Why the little spot? Isn't the spot supposed to be much bigger than this?"

"Yes, it must be bigger. I doubt her virginity. Some man tempered with her body."

Some women from the back of the crowd laughed.

"But that daughter of Hoko had no known boyfriend. We have never seen her with any man."

"So, you think men temper with a woman's body by the path-side? Were you her guard during the night?"

"Women listen, allow me to ask one question. If one is not a virgin, would you see this red spot? Isn't it this is blood? If so, where did it come from?" All of them kept quiet. These were wise words from a reasoning woman. She continued.

"You forget that Hoko does not have a boy child. His daughters do every donkey work that sons should be doing. They are plough handlers, milkers, herders and hut constructors, jobs that are meant for men."

"And donkey riders too." Someone from the crowd added.

"Ooh yes. Especially that one. If a girl child rides on donkey backs and when she marries, you expect a big dot of blood, it is backward. Life is changing these days. Last month Mhizha's son refused a girl from his deceased wife's people. They had given him a wife in replacement of her sister as *chimutsamapfihwa,* where a sister to the deceased marries her sister's husband."

"*Yowee!* Those who are beneath the soil, please help these kids understand our culture." A chorus of disapproval echoed across the little round hut.

"So, they allowed him to refuse her?"

"What were they supposed to do? Rape him? You know you can't rape a man."

"What if his deceased wife's spirit starts haunting either him or the poor chosen girl?"

"Whose fault is that? Of course, you can fight a man with clenched fists, but not a spirit."

"He is thick-headed, but life shall teach him a very good lesson. Does he think all men and women with grey hair who submit to spirits are stupid?"

"Women, you are adding too many subjects here. Now we are losing the head of our intended subject. Who doesn't know Mhizha's sons and daughters are mischievous? Spare us please." The eldest woman brought order in the hut.

"So, we were saying because Hoko's daughter was a donkey rider, this is why her virginity produced a small dot of blood, and she was a virgin before last night."

The women started ululating in jubilation. Men were waiting for this sound of joy outside. Even Punha herself was waiting for the time of her virginity pronouncement. She was glad she had made it. It was an absolute achievement for every young woman in her journey into adulthood. A journey whereby gossipers would stand by and review your history. Once they saw the tatters, they would laugh to tears.

Chapter 12

"Gambiza... *yowee,* why does saliva choke me like this? When am I going to eat delicious food?"

"Master, you make me laugh this morning. You forget Chivi sent a *munyai,* the go-between for Marujata's marriage talks?" Gambiza cackled.

"Gambiza wait. Women are too forgetful, like that donkey which invited its friend hippopotamus to go invade a farmer's field. When the farmer and his sons came chasing them, Donkey ran away but Hippo, being an incompetent sprinter was caught. Donkey knew Hippo was not good at running but wanted him to be beaten. Later on, Hippo learnt the truth. In revenge, he invited Donkey to another farmer's field which was near the riverbanks. The farmer called his servants and chased the two animals. Hippo ran towards the river with Donkey following. Hippo dived into the full river. Donkey followed, but because he could not swim, he drowned. So, woman don't be forgetful like that stupid donkey. We went to the chief's palace and you know Chivi is going to pay Marujata's *rovora* after which we will in turn give it to Mufakose. So, when am I going to eat delicious food when the situation is like that?"

Gambiza frowned as she remembered the chief's verdict on that day.

"You are a good storyteller Master, but did the chief say we give Mufakose all?"

"The chief does not know how much Chivi is going to give us, so we give back to Mufakose his wealth that he gave us and a fine on top. So, when Chivi comes here, we have to charge him more than we owe, if at all we are to be left with surplus."

"That's my wish."

Chivi and his kinsmen gathered. After a meeting that lasted less than an hour, they set for Makoni's homestead. In the procession was Chivi himself, Runesu's mother and other women of the family, Toindepi, Gwenzi, Runesu, Marujata and the rest of the kinsmen. Taruvona the munyai was there also. It was him who was leading all proceedings.

It was an hour's walk from the western end of Gokuda village to Tseisi village. Young men and women would take just half an hour, only that this delegation consisted of mostly old men and women whose bodies' energies had been spent by the passage of time.

The footpath from Gokuda led them towards the stream Gambure where every human, domestic and wild animal drank from. They passed through a dense forest of huge trees, climbers and creepers. It is this forest which was every herbalist's source of raw materials. Carvers also roamed this place in search of fine trees for their carvings.

The footpath meandered downward into the stream. They crossed the stream, leaving their well on the right side. One man from the crowd stopped to take a drink at the well.

"This is the problem of drinking too much beer when you know you are on a journey the following day. How is it possible that a man drinks water during these hours of the morning without having any solid stuff in his stomach?" The man was now rising up from where he had knelt to drink on all fours like an animal.

"Water is good for the body. I am not like Bopoto who says once he has drunk beer he does not take in water because there is water in beer."

"Ooh you mean that mother beater? Where humans are counted it's a sheer waste of time counting him, for it will be like counting mice and their tails."

The procession continued upstream into another little bushy forest. The singing of birds and barking of baboons could be heard here and there. Insects buzzed in the sky as if escorting the Chivi delegation.

Tseisi village was situated on a flat surface near a range of hills called Mharepare. Homesteads were once in line order, but now they spread haphazardly across the village area. This was caused by expansion of families as fathers married more wives and sons got married. A married son was kept at his parent's homestead until his younger brother married, thereafter he was expected to build his own huts close to his parent's. This way, he and his wife were independent from their parents in many aspects. This meant his wife would then cook in her cooking hut and do other feminine chores on her own. The same applied to her husband. He would take full responsibility of his small family, but both submitting to their parents, as the culture dictated.

Makoni's homestead was at the southern outskirts of the village. A footpath led the Chivis straight to the Makoni homestead. From afar, one would see a marked area where the cattle kraal once stood some years ago, before Makoni was seized by demons of destitute and squandered whatever thing was called wealth. Only a small goat pen was visible near this place. The few goats that made this pen a home belonged to Gambiza. Makoni had no livestock of his own. This structure was on the left of the footpath. On its right were three graves, all looking old with no sign of any memorial rite having taken place since their placement. Two of them belonged to Makoni's parents. The third one belonged to his elder brother who died in infancy. Very few villagers knew him, not even Makoni himself. Makoni grew up being told he was the only son of his parents, although a few kinsmen had once told him of his deceased brother, who he seemed to care little about.

Taruvona instructed his delegation to sit down by the bush close to the pen. In accordance with their culture, he was going to consult the Makonis alone and then come back and fetch them if their in-laws had told him so. An enclosure made of thorny branches of trees ran the perimeter of Makoni's homestead. No son had yet built his own huts at the outskirts of his homestead. The enclosure looked old and worn out due to lack of maintenance. During his drinking days, Makoni had no time for such errands. Only Tanaka and his brothers did the work here and there, usually after a request from their mother.

Taruvona walked along the path towards Makoni's yard. Perspiration trickled from his bald head down to his shoulders and chest. He did not wipe the sweat as he considered it harmless. He went through a gap in the enclosure that the Makonis called a gate. Now he was on the periphery of the yard in full view of the several partially maintained huts. He started clapping his hands with much vigour, sending echoes across the yard.

"*Eee* Makoni. The Big Buffalo. Grass-eater. Orphan keeper, the well of life. The ones who crossed Pungwe river and settled in the land of milk and honey."

A handful of boys came and received him. They led him into a hut prepared for sons-in-law.

"Tell your people to pay a token of admission into this homestead."

"Alright Great Buffalo. Let me go and convey the message to them."

On the other end of the yard to the north of the homestead was a big *muchakata* tree that gave shade to people and their fowls. Its fruits, though others said gave an unpleasant smell, to some were edible. The seed was dried and struck to extract nuts from it. During drought, the fruit sap was mixed with mealie-meal to make porridge. Knowing they would receive visitors this day, they had swept and cleaned the area under that tree the previous day. The hut for sons-in-law could not accommodate all members of both families.

The Chivis pledged two goats, ten basketfuls of millet and six hoes, as a token of admission. It was then that they were admitted into Makoni's homestead.

The Chivis walked in a single file with Taruvona leading the way like an army commander. The guests made a half-circle facing their hosts who completed the other half to form a well-designed circumference.

According to Karanga culture, marriage talks for a daughter being married were done by men. Women just sat as part of the audience. The only time they were permitted to say something was when maternal tokens were announced, of which there are few out of all *rovora* instalments. Maternal *rovora* instalments included tokens paid to aunts and grandmothers for bringing up a daughter in good ways of their people; and payments given to the biological mother for the labour pains she suffered during birth of her daughter. The son-in-law considered the latter token a gesture of gratitude to their mother-in-law for bearing a wife for them.

After greetings and introductions, the guests were ushered into Makoni's hut for sons-in-law. The hosts remained behind. Separating the two families was done so that each group freely discussed any opinions without the other hearing their secret views. The *munyai* would frequent the route between the *muchakata* tree and the hut with messages from either side.

The Chivis were first requested to pay a fine for snatching Makoni's daughter in a marriage custom that was despised, though it was common among the Karanga people. The Makonis charged a head of ox which was not disputed. Other marriage procedures followed, with the main rovora payments being the kraal price, where a son-in-law pays a number of heads of cattle. To many people this was the real *rovora*. The Makonis charged fifteen heads of cattle. Initially Makoni and Gambiza wanted twelve heads, but because they knew the rest of the bride price was to be sent to Mufakose they increased their request so that they would be left with a surplus. The Chivis did not hesitate. They actually nodded their heads in agreement. The *munyai* was dashing from one group to the other. Among the heads of cattle for the bride price, there was one head of cattle that was for Gambiza. Yes, Karanga culture dictates that one head of cattle should be given to the biological mother of the girl child married. If the said biological mother is deceased one of her sisters or one of her brother's daughters was given the heifer. Yes, it has to be a heifer that would bear her calves and enlarge her herd. The aunts and grandmother were not forgotten. They got their handsome shares and were all smiles.

The proceedings ended well, leaving everyone happy with the fairness done to both parties. Before they dispersed, they agreed on a date when the Makonis would come and fetch their pledged wealth. The Chivis also informed their in-laws that they would soon come and do the *kusungira* custom. This was done whenever a bride was pregnant. She was sent to stay with her people when she was heavy with child, so that she delivered there within her people. This was a long-kept custom meant to give the bride's people enough time to prescribe and administer remedies that were used by their daughter to smoothen her birth canal for easy baby delivery. Each people used their own herbs that could be different from other people's.

After all the *rovora* proceedings, they all came to the shade of the *muchakata* tree for introductions.

Chapter 13

A fool and his wealth easily part. Taruvona was given a goat and a sheep as a token of gratitude for his *munyai* role, where he was a conveyor of messages between the Makonis and Chivis the day Marujata's rovora was paid. After a week, he had barter traded the sheep with Hoko who wanted to slaughter it and have relish for his family. Mutton was his wife's favourite meat, he had said. Hoko gave him fifteen basketfuls of maize and three basketfuls of rapoko in exchange for the beast. Taruvona wanted to brew beer to appease the spirit of his mother who had died some years ago. His people always said if he did not observe such an important custom, he would know no peace in his entire life.

After that, Tarubva, a villager from Tseisi came demanding that he pay for the beer that he had drunk some months ago. Taruvona had promised to pay soon, which he defaulted. Actually, Taruvona was a bad debtor, but had a sweet tongue. He would skilfully get whatever he wanted so easily, even with a reputation of not honouring his promises. This was known across the whole community.

Tarubva was a talkative woman, very violent when angered or provoked. Taruvona, being a man who hated quarrels, had no option but to give her his goat as payment. One would wonder how huge the volume of beer Taruvona had drunk to incur such a debt. Surely, it was not equivalent to a goat. So, they agreed that Tarubva gave Taruvona a turkey as change.

When Tarubva left pulling the goat by a leash, Taruvona's wife confronted her husband.

"Master, this is not good. You should have kept those two beasts. In three months, they would have reproduced a lamb and a kid each. But now see..."

"Woman, calm down. I am the head of this family. That means all humans living in this homestead are under my authority, including you. You can't give me lectures on how I run my household, unless you want to be a co-ruler with me, which is totally impossible."

"Who said you are not the head of this family? And who wants to be co-ruler with you? All I am saying is other men gather wealth, but you scatter it like fowls do when feeding."

"Other men? I am not 'other men'. They are not me either. Listen woman, these animals were given to me as payment for being a good go-between between two feuding families, a task two other men failed to accomplish. As for the animals, don't worry. I can do the same job for other families any day and get paid again. Then I can slaughter both beasts for you, my wife."

"Master, why is your life full of comedy like this? You can't be serious for just a minute?"

"I am a jovial man who knows that such speeches make life easy. Even the day I proposed love to you, you said "yes" before I had completed a single statement of courtship."

"Liar! That's pure lies. Was I a whore that is proposed directly with no *gwevedzi* as your aid?"

"Woman, you don't say a man is lying, but you say what he is saying is untrue."

"And what is the difference?"

"The difference lays in the manner in which you say it."

"Master. You are too much." Tarubva giggled.

"You see, now you are laughing."

In Makoni's homestead, several events took place that same month. It was their busiest month. They went to Chief Mposi's court for the marriage triangle settlement. The Chivis came to pay for Marujata's *rovora*, bride price. In the same month, the Chivis came with what they had pledged at the marriage talk. The Makonis gave Mufakose what he was owed and topped up with a fine of two heads of cattle. They kept the surplus for themselves. They gave the other beast to the chief as he had demanded on the court day.

Mufakose accepted his wealth back, but he was not happy at all. He visibly showed his anger to everyone who was there. The entire community ended up knowing his disapproval of the chief's verdict. Had Makoni given him another of his daughters, maybe he could have cooled his temper. At the chief's palace he had openly told the audience that no amount of wealth would quench his anger. He could not be swayed to accept Chivi's apology.

Time flies like a bird of prey. The surplus was three heads of cattle, which Makoni and his family sent a *munyai*, go-between, to invoke Hoko and his family into marriage talks. The munyai was well received in Hoko's homestead. A date was set for talks. Makoni and his family set off for a short journey northward in the same village where Hoko lived with his wife. His homestead was a small dwelling with a few huts. His *hozi* or father's house was the most outstanding feature, like a big cock among a flock of hens and chicks. Although many men bragged about their wealth of multiple wives, children and livestock, Hoko was just a simple man content in his religious role. To him, that role overrode every title a man could have ambitions for. One would just imagine if headmen, herbalists, and other villagers used to report to his homestead for revelations and clarity on hidden matters of the community, then he was a great man. Only the chief would send a messenger for the spirit man. His was the highest office between men and spirits.

When a daughter gets married, she is not only married to her husband, but to the whole family of her husband, so goes the Karanga culture. And if a son marries someone's daughter, it is not only him who is a son-in-law in the family of his wife. The entire extended family automatically becomes sons-in-law. It is the responsibility of the father to pay *rovora* for his sons, unless the son is a man of means, which is unlikely, considering the son's age. A man acquires wealth after working for it for a considerable period of time, unless he inherits it from his parents. This was usually the case when a man was marrying a first wife. As for the second wife and multiple others, the man was considered adult enough not to seek his parent's aid in *rovora*. That's the Karanga culture.

The Makonis paid *mapinzo* which is a *rovora* instalment used as an admission ticket into the Hoko homestead. It was then that they were allowed in the yard. As the proceedings continued, they paid *makandihwanani,* which was a token for asking the sons-in-law how they came to know Hoko was the father of their bride. For *mapinzo* the Makonis pledged three goats, two heads of cattle for *makandihwanani*. Of the three heads of cattle they had at their homestead, one was a heifer which they politely requested to pay as the maternal beast that was given to the mother-in-law, which was granted. The other head of cattle, an ox was given to the father-in-law as part of the herd given to the biological father of the married daughter. At this stage the Makonis were left with nothing more. One of the eldest members of the Hoko family asked why they had pledged inadequate wealth. The munyai coolly explained.

"Excuse us *Mhukahuru*. You know what our children put us into these days is very unpredictable. This was like a hare that jumps from its hiding place through a hunter's legs. He cannot hit it with any of his weapons. Our daughter-in-law eloped to our son without his knowledge."

"You mean *kuganha* is what she did?"

"Yes, *Mhukahuru*. Yes, Great Elephant. Thorn eater. Tree twister."

"It's alright, after all when our sons and daughters marry, they join us as one big extended family. When we accept your *rovora* it does not mean we are greedy people who sell their daughter in order to be rich. No people can become rich by marrying off their daughters. Wealth of men comes from their innocent perspiration. *Rovora* is a token of appreciation between two families. Actually, our people say you don't pay *rovora* for a wife in a single day. What if she is barren? What if you catch her with another man in your matrimonial bed? What if she is a witch or a lazy woman?"

Guests were served a variety of dishes of sadza and meat. Sadza made of rapoko, millet, maize meal and rice. Beef, chicken and goat meat were in abundance. *Mukumbi*, the marula drink, which was one day old, was brought forward as dessert. No man could get drunk by drinking one-day old *mukumbi*. They all ate and drank, chatting happily like people of one big family.

Tanaka was becoming fond of Punha. At first, he had that feeling of an ox towards a cow. But adults are smart. You don't put two creatures of different sex in one enclosure and expect nothing to take place. Lust will start to germinate and develop into love. Now the two lovebirds could be seen chatting together, laughing and shaking hands.

Punha was the kind of woman you would not like if you don't take time to understand. She was neither beautiful, nor could she be said to be ugly. A lady of medium height and stout with smooth ebony skin. Her height was not proportional to Tanaka's, for he was as tall as a spook. Rarely do you see a short spook, villagers said.

In spite of her facial features and body structure, Punha was a workaholic. She dreaded no work, be it work suitable for men or women, she was a champion of both. She was an excellent milker, land tiller, roof thatcher, herder, mealie pounder, mealie grinder, cook, hut cleaner, yard sweeper all bundled in one. Because her father had no sons, he had taught his daughters all kinds of jobs. For this reason, Punha's in-laws Gambiza and Makoni liked her. Even other members of the extended family liked her.

Chapter 14

Time moved with seasons rolling over, years galloping like excited calves in a grazing field. Marujata was sent to her family in accordance with the *kusungira* marriage custom. She gave birth to a bouncing baby boy.

"Look at his nostrils. Wide-open like his father's."

"And the charcoal black complexion shows he is really a Chivi boy. No Chivi person is pale. All are black like sets of pots."

"But the ears and eyes are his mother's."

Women exchanged chats in a hut that was full of women only. No man was allowed in it. Not even the biological father was permitted to peer from outside. It was taboo. It was only after the baby's umbilical cord had dried up and fallen off that he was then allowed to get out of the hut. That is when all members of the family could come with presents to give to the new family member. The umbilical cord was kept in a secret place and later buried during the night.

At this stage the baby had no name. After a family consultation meeting, they agreed on one name. His grandfather Chivi called him Takunda. After all the quarrels that involved three families, quarrels that ended at the chief's court, where they, the Chivis were acquitted, it was a fitting name. Takunda, a Karanga word that means 'we have won'. Chivi gave his grandson two goats. Anyone who felt the name must be changed had to give away more than what he had offered. Nobody raised a finger of protest, so the name stood.

The boy grew up healthy from the time of breastfeeding, to crawling, to walking and talking. It was then that Marujata was seen heavy, with another pregnancy. You don't keep a single baby. You give him a sibling as soon as possible. Men love women who bear many children more than those who don't.

"Why are you troubling your son like that? Look he is seated there like an eaglet in a nest with no sibling to play with?" Her mother had said this to her on one of her visits to her daughter.

Virimayi was Tanaka's half-brother. The two being both sons of Makoni. The boy's mother was Makoni's second wife, but Makoni had divorced him some years ago. She was fed up of constant beatings that she received for asking why he was wasting everything that the family owned. She had been the only outspoken one among Makoni's four wives back then. Because she came from a well up family, she could not stand the abuse and later on the abject poverty the family was subjected to when all wealth was gone.

This boy Virimayi was her mother's first-born child, followed by Sekai and three more. The third wife had given Makoni two kids, both boys. The same abuse made her say 'enough is enough'. Very few women could be bold enough to resort to divorce. The fourth and last wife had no children. She went the same way. Meetings were done between each of the women's families and that of Makoni, to find common ground and try to redress the situation. Because of his character of no remorse and impolite speeches, nothing was solved. Makoni could not be drawn into accepting his wrongdoing. To himself he was always perfect.

Virimayi was in talks with Mhizha's daughter, Haruna. He loved her although he knew his father had nothing to give to Mhizha as *rovora*. Haruna also loved Virimayi despite his family's poverty. Virimayi was a hard-working young man who was handsome and usually quiet. He was never found in the wrong path, like other young men of the village. A wrong could be done without his name ever being mentioned.

Mhizha was not a poor man. Neither was he a rich man. His family was well sustained with no complaints of insufficient food and basic needs. His two wives wore the best attires at village gatherings; they were the envy of other villagers.

Haruna was from the second wife, pale in complexion, slender and walked with knock-kneed legs. Her sexy dimples were an added icing on top of her beauty. A gap between her front teeth gave her a distinct facial feature that made her unforgettable.

One Wednesday, Virimayi visited Nhonho, his uncle. He had a cock under his armpit. Nhonho was a cousin brother to Makoni, the former being younger than the latter. Their fathers were brothers

"Uncle, I have a challenging issue here that needs your advice. You are the one who saw the sun earlier than me, and every word you say is of importance to a boy with milk on his nose like me."

"These are ears son. They are ever open for listening." Nhonho said with both his palms on his ears.

"Thank you, uncle." Virimayi fidgeted visibly, showing difficulty in finding a way with which to break his news.

"Uncle ummm...."

"Virimayi my son, your uncle is here with his ears at attention. Be free and speak up."

"Uncle, I am here to tell you that I think I am old enough."

Nhonho knew what Virimayi meant. If a son said he was old enough, it meant he was intending to marry. The old man kept quiet for a while and coughed to clear his throat.

"Whose daughter are you seeing?"

"Mhizha's. Mhizha of Matando village."

"Of course, in accordance with our culture, I will inform my brothers about it, but as you know it is the responsibility of the father to pay *rovora* for his son. Your father, my brother has nothing in his homestead. What Chivi gave him was in turn given to Mufakose to settle a long-standing dispute that ended at the chief's court. The little that was left over as you know was used as *rovora* for your brother's wife, the daughter of Hoko. Now as it is there is nothing left. Even so, there was no way Marujata's wealth could be used by anyone other than her brothers born from the same womb. Were it that Sekai was married, your father could take her *rovora* and give it to your in-laws because both of you were born from the same womb. That's the custom, I think you know this."

"Yes, uncle I know this, but I was thinking about something."

"Then tell me what's on your mind."

"Our people have a marriage custom called *kutema ugariri* where a boy from a poor family can go and work for his future wife in the homestead of his in-laws."

"*Hezvo* Virimayi! Is that what you have decided to do?"

"Uncle, I don't have any alternative. I can't wait to marry Sekai. What if she marries someone else after five years of waiting? Or what if she never marries."

"No, don't say that. Don't wish her bad."

"I am not wishing her bad uncle. It's something which is possible. Actually, it is also good for a man to pay for his wife's *rovora*."

"If that's your plan son, I will inform my brothers as I told you. When do you think we can approach the Mhizhas?"

"Next week."

"*Hezvo*! So soon? Why do you behave like you are in a race to marry?"

"Uncle, an animal hide is folded when it's wet. And a metal is beaten hot."

"Children of today. So, you think marriage is that easy like cutting butter with a hot knife on a hot day? Age is nothing, but maturity is everything." He chuckled.

"l have both, uncle."

"It's alright son, if you are daring enough. But don't think if you are able to speak in proverbial expressions that you are old enough. A man is not judged by the size of his head but by the senses in it."

"Thank you, uncle. Here is your present I brought you."

"Thank you, my son. Now I can see you are old enough. You don't come with your stories before adults empty-handed like a defeated general."

The following week a family meeting was conducted in Zenda's homestead, the eldest member in the Makoni family. Nhonho informed other elders what their son was up to. They all agreed without much contention that *kutema ugariri* was the most appropriate way out. They sent a *munyai* to summon the Mhizhas. A date for the marriage talks was set.

At the meeting, the Mhizhas accepted the Makoni's request.

"Our son is a strong man. I trust he will not disappoint both of us. We look forward to seeing him completing his task as agreed. We reckon you are going to be proud of him."

"That's the wish of every parent, to see his son growing up to be able to sustain his family. That's the beginning of a new journey for both of them. We know your son is a guest now. After that it's my daughter who shall be a guest in your family. Such is the irony of life."

Two weeks passed after the meeting between the Makonis and the Mhizhas took place. Virimayi was sent to live with the Mhizhas. There, he was treated as Mhizha's son. Mhizha was his father, Mhizha's wife his mother. Their children were his siblings. All Mhizha's daughters were his sisters, and his sons were brothers. Even his wife-to-be was his sister. Never was he allowed to say something to do with love to her. The two were not allowed to meet secretly. The girls' hut and its proximity were a no-go zone. For five years, the rules stood as the custom of *kutema ugariri* dictated.

Virimayi was an obedient son. He would do anything he was ordered to do with no element of complaint. Before he came to live with the Mhizhas, Mhizha was just a moderate man in terms of wealth. He was not really a great farmer. Neither was he a poor farmer. Everything about him was average. When Virimayi came, that same year, Mhizha filled two big barns of maize and millet. Two more neat huts were constructed by Virimayi himself. He did not mind whether his brothers assisted or not. The cattle kraal and pens for sheep and goats were transferred to fresher ground. New yokes, mortars and pestles, stools and wooden cooking utensils were carved. He made baskets, mats and drums. Sometimes he would bring meat from his hunting expeditions with other men, fish from the river and he killed birds for his new family. He removed the old enclosure to the homestead and made a new secure one with two gates on opposite sides. He also built a new fowl run and wooden table at a place where women washed cooking utensils. The table was for laying the utensils on so that they dry before they carry them into the kitchen. He rethatched all the huts in the homestead.

Mhizha's homestead was now a magnificent residence. Every villager admired it. Virimayi became the talk of the village.

"The boy from Tseisi village is very hardworking. I wish he would finish working for his wife."

"Then you do what?"

"Then I give him my daughter as a second wife. Yes. My daughter would not starve with such a strong husband."

"You are crazy. What if he does not love your daughter?"

"There is nothing like that. Where have you seen a man who refuses a woman given to him as a wife? Our culture does not allow that. From the headman, chief, and King Munhumutapa to the gods of this land they all know it's taboo." One would overhear some women talking about Virimayi. Others would go as far as wondering why Makoni's homestead had dilapidated huts, yet he had such a hardworking son. You would hear someone say, "Makoni has many sons, why that boy alone. It is him who is a passive leader," they would conclude.

The following year, Mhizha had a bumper harvest again. One of his two big barns was extended to accommodate millet. His wives had each a barn of small grains like groundnuts, roundnuts and beans. Food was plenty that year, they had to trade the old grains of the previous year with other villagers.

Virimayi became the darling of the village. Everyone liked him except for one boy who lived within the village. He had been the first one to send a *gwevedzi*, intermediator to Haruna. When the beautiful lady was about to give in, then came Virimayi, as swift as lightning and was quickly accepted. Maybe Virimayi's *gwevedzi* was more active than that boy's. An intermediator needs not be too casual. It was his skilful ability that his sender banked on.

Chapter 15

In life, the sun will rise and set, weeks pass by, seasons come and go, and a year ends and another begins. Events happen here and there, some unexpected and unpredictable, whereas others are sure to happen each year at their rightful time.

Bopoto had run away to an unknown place after he was accused of raping a pregnant woman in Matando village. When the chief sent his guards to arrest him, he vanished into thin air. No news of his whereabouts was heard afterwards.

Chinjanja, Runesu's grandmother died in her sleep. Her granddaughters, with whom she shared a room, knew nothing of her death until early morning of that day when Runesu's mother entered the hut in search of her missing sickle. It was then that she found the old lady's body cold. It was old age. "No, some goblin visited her during her sleep," villagers said in whispers.

She was buried next to her husband's grave at the family cemetery. After a week, the whole family visited a diviner to find out what had eaten their loved one. After a year, beer to bring into the family the spirit of the old woman was brewed. She had lived all her years well among her people. The gods had been good to her. She bore nine children, five daughters and four sons, had numerous grandchildren and great-grandchildren. No family member or villager knew her exact age, but there was no argument that she had been the oldest member of the family. She had been a good instructor to her husband's junior wives, culture enforcer and storyteller to her grandchildren, everybody remembered. Now she had left the land of the humans and was automatically elevated into the land of spirits so that her spirit, after being brought back, was able to look after the family. Its guidance and protection were expected as was the culture. Any spirit is good as long as you do not offend it. In the unlikely event that a spirit was offended, the family would consult a diviner who would explain how the appeasement should be done, the appropriate manner that would satisfy the offended spirit.

Marujata now had three children, two boys and a girl, all born in quick succession, each year after she became wife to Runesu. The way Runesu and Marujata reproduced, one would think they were in a race with other young couples of the village where the winner was given the moon and all stars of the asteroid belt.

Makoni was now a changed man. He seldom drank beer. His association with Taruvona and other nuisances of the community was cut short. Now he wanted to correct every mistake that he had done, he had emphasized to anybody who cared to listen to him.

"You cannot be great by associating with ordinary men. What do they impart on you other than spending precious time doing unproductive things? Life is emulated from others. Others that are great in life. Look at a great man with admiration not jealousy. Tell yourself that nothing done by someone born of a woman is impossible." Zenda, his cousin brother, had convincingly told him.

Little was known or said about Mufakose since the chief's court. He had lived a low-profile life since that day. Even Makoni had never heard any news from him and his friend Jekanyika, for the relationship was cut by the chief on that court day. Villagers from the eastern and western ends would meet at annual festivals. Even then, there would be so many people one would find no place to spit saliva, let alone recognize a person who was of less importance.

Zvidzai got married in the last year of Virimayi's stay in Matando village. As according to culture, Tanaka was given a place to build his huts by his father. The place was to the east of his father's homestead but within the same proximity. No two married sons were kept in their father's homestead unless resources or other factors hindered the sequence of a son growing into adulthood. In such circumstances, a mutual understanding was observed between all parties involved, parents, son and daughter-in-law.

Sekai got a man from a faraway village. They met at an annual festival, villagers said. But her family was not happy with the geographic location of her husband's village.

"Children of today are very mischievous. Aunts and grandmothers spend years teaching and advising them on the ways of our people. You see them quiet as if they are attentive, but alas, words enter with this ear and get out through the other." Zenda emphasized his speech by gestures, with hands moving from his right ear to his left.

"Marry within your community. Marry within your community, this we always preach, but they don't listen. Now tell me, do we know how people in that community live? Or do they know our ways of life either? You see, these children with their thick-headedness one day will marry children of our enemies or marry from people who despise our gods, then you will realize it's equal to giving itching eyes a remedy of pepper."

It seemed people from Sekai's husband knew her family was likely to refuse to bless their daughter's marriage, so they moved quickly. Slowness is familiar to a leopard, a hyena eats as it moves, so goes the Karanga proverb.

They paid everything that was asked for to the last item. After two days from the marriage talks, they called their in-laws to come to their place and select their cattle among their herds, something that was unheard of back in Mposi community.

During Virimayi's stay in Matando village, his biological mother visited him once every year coming from her people. During each visit, she would take time to speak to her daughter-in-law to-be. The two created a strong bond, even before Virimayi and Haruna became husband and wife.

In his final year, Virimayi asked Mhizha to excuse him for a few days. He wanted to go and chat with his family, particularly his father. Since he was older than Zvidzai, he had no place in his father's homestead. Only the youngest son was allowed to reside in his father's homestead. From the eldest son, each son would substitute the older one in that order until the last-born son remained. This one was not allowed to leave his father's homestead. It was his duty to look after the parents who were ageing each passing year.

Virimayi's plea was granted. His father and uncles were happy to see him. He was shown his place and started building two huts of poles and mud, with grass-thatched roofs. His two younger brothers born of the same mother helped him. After four days he was done. He went back to Matando village and finished his tenure.

The Mhizhas sent a messenger to the Makonis informing them of the day they would perform a send-off ceremony. The two families agreed on a Wednesday which was a non-working day. Of all the seven days of the week, Wednesday was a day set aside by the gods of the land as the resting day. Working in the fields on this day was an offence punishable by a fine set by the chief. Only work done in homesteads and anywhere else other than the farming fields was allowed.

When the day arrived Haruna was dressed in colourful Karanga attire and her body decorated with the best colours known by the costumiers of the family. Virimayi also did his best to look as good as he could. Haruna's aunts led the procession heading for Tseisi village. Other members of the family, neighbours and friends of the family were part of the crowd. Women balanced pots of beer on their heads and men were pulling two goats by means of leashes. Others had drums and trumpets.

In Tseisi village, the Makonis were waiting for their guests. The entire Makoni homestead was spotless clean. Neighbours could be seen peering through apertures on their huts, apertures that served as windows. Anything good is likeable, no man hates a good thing, the Karanga people say.

Chibadura was already there. Now nobody wondered why he was ever present or who invited him. They knew people of Chibadura's character did not wait for invitation. They invited themselves wherever they were found. Sometimes Chibadura would go to a place of such magnitude without knowing why people had gathered. Like what he did one year when Headman Matando was welcoming his son-in-law and daughter who had come for a *mapinzo* ceremony. He mistook the event for a funeral. He picked one of the drums and started a sorrowful song familiar with funerals. He beat the drum as usual with his high-pitched voice on top of every sound. A certain villager of Matando gave him a pat on the shoulder and whispered.

"Chibadura, this is not a funeral. It's a welcome ceremony for Headman Matando's son-in-law and daughter."

It was then that he stopped the song, showing a pinch of shame.

The procession of the Mhizhas was well received by the Makonis. Their two huts were readily available, one for men and the other for women. After a short while, after greetings where the munyai was the conductor of the ceremony, the guests were given food. After eating, all guests and hosts were ushered to the Makoni yard outside. No room could accommodate all of them. Introductions were done. After that, Zenda stood up and spoke. He thanked the gods of the land for the gift of life and health, the rulers of their kingdom for maintaining peace and tranquillity among their people. He then thanked their in-laws for doing them a favour by bearing such a beautiful daughter only to give to them as a wife. He also said he hoped his son was now an adult to understand the duties of a man. He wished his two children wonderful prosperous lives, full of grandsons, so that the Makoni name lived long, and granddaughters who would grow up to be aunts and would in turn teach all female members of the family ways of their people. That way their culture would remain intact. He rounded off his speech by repeating the same proverb recited at every marriage ceremony, that "marriage was their people's way of extending relationships".

When Zenda sat down, one man who looked like he was the oldest man of the Mhizha family stood up. He first saluted his hosts and then thanked the gods of the land and all revered traditional leaders of the community. He thanked everybody who was present for his or her precious time saved for that event. He went on to thank the Makonis for bringing up a hardworking and strong son.

"Ever since he became part of our family five years ago, he did not disappoint. He would do all assigned tasks wholeheartedly without questioning anything. Actually, most of his duties were self-thought. If we the Mhizhas are to be honest with you all here, this young man who I can proudly say is now our son-in-law is a man none of us taught anything. He knew his duties and did them with no supervision. We don't see our daughter and grandchildren, which I am sure the god of fertility will provide us with, dying of starvation with such a husband and father. Wealth is nothing to a fool, but the little a wiseman has is more valuable that what a fool has. Manners, hardworking and senses build a man. It is a pity he had to take this marriage route of *kutema ugariri*. If he had paid *rovora* by bringing wealth to us, I swear with my departed ancestors we would have given him a second wife plucked from among our many daughters. Yes, a good son-in-law is as valuable as gold. I wish you well my children. Long lives to both of you. Reproduce like others. Let us hold our grandchildren on our laps before we die. A parent who has seen his grandchildren can safely join his or her ancestors in the land of spirits with no grievance. Seeing your great-grandchildren like Nyatsimba Mutota did is a bonus that comes when gods have smiled at you." He concluded.

When the old man ended his speech a round of applause punctuated with whistles and ululating swept the arena.

After every speaker had poured out his thoughts, the crowd dispersed, roaming around the yard. This was

Chibadura's time to show his prowess. His drum beating was so excellent that even a man with a bruised leg would try a step-in dancing. The dancing would stop here and there when people were ordered to sit in groups of three or four as food and drink was served to them.

Chapter 16

A man who is used to his trade, a man who has amassed enough experience in his trade that whenever he is in it, he does every stage of it with passion, rarely is able to change into another trade. Such was the case with Runesu. He remained a hunter as before. Now with many years' experience of doing the same thing over and over, he was now a specialist in hunting. He would tell from the footprints which animal had passed through that area, at what approximate time, where it was heading and whether it was female or male. He could distinguish one animal sound from another easily, even those which sounded slightly similar. His snares seldom missed an animal that stepped on it. The forest was part of his home, familiar with every bush, creeper, climber and tree in it. Even the way he navigated his way from home to his haphazardly placed snares and back again, was a result of amazing knowledge and instincts.

Runesu's small yard near his father's homestead, which comprised two huts that he was made to build after his young brother got married, was a butchery in itself. Meat from different animals was always there, dried and fresh. The yard suited him well as a man of lion totem. His wife and sister were always busy slicing and drying meat and storing it in skinbags of different volumes. It is this meat that brought wealth for Runesu. He would barter trade with anyone for anything he wanted. His whole family depended on him for meat that he generously parcelled to each one of them.

On one of his hunting expeditions, Runesu encountered a situation that nearly ended his life. He found a lion on his snare about to eat a kudu caught on it. The big cat came for a counterattack. Runesu being the greatest hunter of Mposi village looked at it straight into its eyes. The beast roared as it charged towards him. The hunter stood almost transfixed at one point; spear firmly held with both hands. He did not wink as the animal leapt forward, missing him by a whisker and landing on the ground after he swayed his body to avoid it. With a quick turn, which the lion also did, they were now facing each other again. The lion roared, now fiercer than before, but Runesu did not budge, with legs astride so that he would not lose his footing. The beast leapt again and Runesu aimed his spear on its neck from the bottom side of his body. The tip of the spear tore its skin. A wound oozing blood was visible, and it brought the animal to a state of ferocity. It frantically charged forward like a blind bull, all canines out for a bite. Runesu now knew it was to his advantage that the animal was wounded. As he retreated, he withdrew his knobkerrie and watched as it came. He struck its head once, twice, thrice. On his fourth blow the animal knelt on its forelegs, pain getting the better of it. Runesu withdrew the knobkerrie and took his spear again. The animal was now groaning on the ground. He stabbed it on its front quarter. The spear pierced through its ribcage. This was the stab that knocked life out of the wild cat. Fighting a wild animal was a game Runesu enjoyed. Not a single bite could be seen on his flesh ever since he became a hunter. This was why villagers of Mposi had it that a hunter's spirit was upon him whenever he was in the forests. One of his departed ancestors was a great hunter. It was his spirit that was upon his great grandson, villagers maintained.

Runesu stood for a while, staring at the dying animal to ensure it was dead. Eventually, the lion took its last breath. He was now tired from the fight that had taken close to an hour. He carried the carcass home, and his friends Toindepi and Gwenzi returned to the forest to help him carry the carcass of the kudu.

News that Runesu son of Chivi killed a lion went public across the community of Mposi. They skinned the animal, then sent for Gumhai the chief's messenger. They gave him the skin of the animal to give to the chief as was according to culture. No ordinary man was allowed to put on attires made of hides of a lion, leopard, cheetah or any valuable animal.

One animal which was considered sacred such that only chiefs were allowed to eat its meat was a pangolin. It was a precious animal for chiefs and traditional leaders only.

The chief, excited by seeing the lion skin and the story of a young man from the Chivi family, asked for the young man and his family to see him. When they arrived at the chief's palace, the chief expressed words of gratitude to the man of courage, Runesu.

"Rarely do you see such courage from a young man like yours. Boys of today who grow up in war-free empires are cowards. Too womanish, one would wonder what will happen to us the day an enemy invades our land."

To top up his gratitude, the chief gave Runesu one of his daughters to be his second wife. The family thanked the chief and left in joy.

Mufakose was known by his family as a disciplinarian who enforced his measures with no regrets. He would get annoyed by a wife or child when they transgressed his set regulations. It was then that his spirit usually got broken.

Since the time he attended the court trial at the chief's palace, to the time he was refunded his wealth by Makoni, Mufakose was a changed man. He seldom showed his teeth in a happy mood. His wives knew he was unhappy with his failure to bring back Marujata.

"How can a man demand a woman carrying another man's child in her womb as a wife?" His second wife asked in total amazement.

"Don't you see he has never been the same since he returned from the chief's palace that year? How can a man be sad all these years? Why can't he dismiss such things as bygones and move on? You would think that Makoni lady has two genitals and two wombs that produce a set of triplets each." The unpredictable Mai Simba reasoned. The other women laughed and clapped hands at Mai Simba's silly jokes.

"Mai Simba, we know you. You were siding with Master that year when we were all against him. Now why this sudden change of heart? Do you want to spy on us, *hee*? Women be careful of Mai Simba; she is a serpent."

Chihera, Mufakose's fourth wife was always constructive in her shrewdness, especially when the occasion presented an opportunity to suppress her. Mai Simba and this woman were not the best of friends.

Mufakose had not seen Runesu since their court day. Neither had he seen Marujata who villagers said had filled her hut with children, a sign that meant she was now a permanent member of the Chivi family. Even when he saw her pregnant at the chief's palace, he quickly knew that reversing whatever had happened was impossible. How can a man reverse nature's circle of events? This made him choke with anger. Accepting an apology from a man who willingly wronged him was a sign of cowardice.

"We shall see. Yes, we shall see. I am not a toddler to be blindfolded by a lame appeasement. This is an open declaration of war with me. One man must fall. Yes, one man must sink." Mufakose spoke to himself one day.

He knew Runesu was a hunter. He used to go on solo hunting trips in Pindaufe forest. Pindaufe was a distant forest away from any village. Few men dared set foot in it. This forest was home to lions and other dangerous wild animals. Many strangers were killed by these animals when they tried to pass through it unknowingly. Just a few hunters would enter this dense forest and come out unscathed. The rest would unfortunately join their ancestors in painful deaths. Pindaufe is a self-explanatory Karanga name that means "enter and die".

During the spring of that year, Mufakose spent much of his time hunting down Runesu. He was examining his travel patterns, how, when and where he spent much of his time.

"His time is up." He had said to himself one day, when he saw him armed from tooth to nail as he set out for his hunting adventures. In terms of physique, Mufakose could not match Runesu even with bare hands. So, confronting him directly was like entering into a lion's den and starting a fight with it; fighting the invincible. Tempering with fire, saying "fire you can't burn me!"

Mufakose had to think of a plan. That day, he followed Runesu half-way. His sixth sense told him to go back home and think again, scratch his head in search of new ideas. The Karanga people say, "If you decide to eat a dog then eat a male bulldog, not a papillon; so that when people laugh at you, you have no shame." It would be of no sense to be laughed at for eating a small dog like a papillon. Mufakose had to dare enough.

A week passed with Mufakose still stalking Runesu. This he kept a secret to himself. Even his good friend, Jekanyika was in the dark. He did not let him know. He did not want anyone to tell him that what he intended doing was a crime and abomination to the gods of the land.

Times were nearing the end of October, the tenth month of the year. Still, there was no sign of the rains. One would wake up to see fleecy clouds that were associated with springtime. Transparent clouds that looked light with no colour of rain were everywhere in the blue sky. That month ended and November, the eleventh month started. November was the month of goat reproduction, where those lucky with goat rearing saw their nanny-goats giving birth to two or three kids. Still, no rain had touched the ground. The sound of thunder and the flickering light of lightning was now remote to every villager. Actually, the villagers had a blunt memory. Not late in spring, Gomwe the seer of the community had foretold that the ancestral spirits were angry with the people. A lot of vices had been committed with no appeasement done. As a result, there would not be any rain soon, unless beer to invoke and appease the spirits of the land was brewed, Gomwe preached. Hoko kept quiet after hearing that. The two, Gomwe and Hoko were not the best of friends. There had been occasions when Hoko felt Gomwe was intruding in his faculty. Each had his own job outlined clearly to any villager. Gomwe was just a seer. He had the ability to foretell future events that were always unknown to ordinary villagers and other traditional leaders. Hoko was a rainmaker. It was him who was the conductor of *mutoro*, a ceremony where beer for spirit appeasement was brewed and rituals done.

During a year like this, where rains were predictably assumed to be less, Hoko's duty was to consult the spirit medium at Mabweadziva shrine.

Mabweadziva was an ancestral shrine in the western area of the Munhumutapa Empire where 'talking' stones were consulted. A rainmaker would, after reaching the shrine, plead with the sacred spirit, which would reply through the huge rocks there. The rainmaker would hear a hoarse voice from the stones narrating what should be done, which he would convey to the traditional leaders of the areas affected, who in turn informed their people.

"Hoko is just a rainmaker whereas I am a seer. He cannot claim to do both jobs by himself. He is being selfish and greedy." Gomwe had said to the villagers.

"I cannot claim to be a rainmaker, but you have known me for years as a seer. Can't men of this community draw a line between my job and Hoko's, which is that simple. A potter and blacksmith are two different craftsmen." The traditional leader emphasized.

Hoko was as quiet and harmless as a dove, never got himself in the war of words with Gomwe, never commented either. But the pressure from villagers already sensing drought and its effects of starvation and livestock deaths looming gave Hoko a headache he could not conceal. If such a calamity was to hit the land, something the people considered to be evitable by spiritual appeasement, they would not be able to forgive him. It was the duty of a rainmaker to make sure all necessary rituals pertaining to rain seasons were done prior to the farming season. If people had erred here and there, it was still his duty to see how they made sacrifices to the gods of the land.

Chapter 17

There still were no rains in the beginning of November, the eleventh month of the year. There was no way Hoko would ignore calls from all villagers for a *mutoro*. All he had asked from them was an understanding that he knew his job well, having done it for years with passion. He considered it disrespectful when they had to hear it from Gomwe that a *mutoro* ceremony was to be done. He needed no reminding from anyone from anywhere, for he feared and respected the spirits of the land that he was in communion with every year, Hoko puffed with anger.

"When trouble wants to hit a certain land, you see it through religious leaders fighting a war of supremacy with no one really paying attention to people's grievances. We did not choose you into those positions, but the spirits ordained you, so do the job with no complaints." One old man of Makotore village told Hoko straight to his face. Hoko left the meeting without saying a word after the old man's speech. Words without deeds are not productive. Spirits are not appeased by words only. *Neither do words till the land*, Hoko told himself as he headed for his homestead.

That same month of goat reproduction, Hoko sent his messengers to go door to door asking for grains to brew beer. In two days, enough had been gathered from each household. Men brought big logs of firewood, women carried water for beer brewing. Three old women past the age of childbearing were recruited. Their fame of being excellent beer makers was sufficient qualification for the job.

From the beginning of its brewing to the end when it was said to be ready for drinking, it lasted seven days. On the first day, Hoko and his assistants left for Mabweadziva. There were five of them with no weapons and they carried no food for the journey. The spirits of the land would provide for its servants, elders said each year.

For seven days they were on a journey to and from the sacred shrine. On the seventh day when everyone was patiently waiting for their return, heavy clouds started building in the sky. It started as a drizzle until more darker clouds rolled over, bringing frightening lightning and thunder. Bigger drops followed. Everyone took refuge in huts and sheds after cooperatively lifting all containers of beer, because there were many people in Hoko's homestead, all waiting for the ceremonial ritual to take place.

From beyond the cattle kraal, Hoko and his delegation appeared, wet and exhausted. Villagers forgot about the rain and leapt in jubilation. Men blew whistles of joy and women ululated with excitement, the noise competing with the rumbling sounds from the clouds was loud enough to alert other villagers who had gone to their homes.

As they entered the yard, bigger drops accompanied by winds beat down. That day it rained cats and dogs. To say it rained would be an understatement; one could precisely say, it poured.

"Yes, that's it. Our ancestors have answered our prayers. Yes, the rain must erase their footsteps as according to custom." One elder reminded others as he stood amid the rain, as if to request it to wash his body with its deluge.

The rain subsided after several hours of lashing down. It was now evening and drums had started sounding in different tunes. Trumpets were blown as people started dancing and singing. Dancers were already dressed in dancing gear, choreographing with passion.

The only missing ingredient of the jubilation was Chibadura. He had suddenly fallen sick with a fever. His associates had brought a herbalist to him and was now in a much better state, villagers had said. Other drummers tried to fill the void left by the best drummer of the community, but no one could really fit squarely.

Mufakose had nothing to do with the *mutoro* ceremony. His presence or absence had no significance in the annual ceremony, he told himself. He was still finding ways with which to deal with Runesu. He would not stop trying new methods until he had succeeded.

That planting season, he got no sight of Runesu because all families were busy in the fields. Runesu would go hunting on Wednesdays only, since they were not working days. Even so, he would not go very far away because forests were very dense with vegetation. Good hunting is done in springtime.

Mufakose could not find a way through to execute his plans. But still, he was optimistic an opportunity would arise one day. His heart would not be at rest as long as one of them, Runesu or him was alive. Not both of them should live but only one must survive the war, the other must die. How Mufakose called it a war was baffling. Runesu was in utter darkness while he was busy crafting evil methods of revenge in his head. If he was man enough, why did he not confront Runesu face to face instead of laying an ambush like a lion stalking an impala.

Bopoto had not yet returned. Rumours said he had run away to a faraway land where he presented himself to a certain rich man as a slave. How he found it better to flee from his motherland and be a slave in a land his people had no knowledge of, shocked everyone. How he had had the audacity to let them pierce his nose as a mark of ownership to his keeper was something everybody found silly. That permanent mark of slavery meant he had no intention of ever setting foot in his homeland again.

Makoni's homestead had grown into a bigger expanded home with several huts surrounding his *hozi*, father's house. Virimayi's and Tanaka's structures were like wings on their father's main homestead, with Zvidzai's two new huts adding value to the little complex. Yes, a man's wealth was judged by the size of his homestead, apart from his wives, children and livestock. Tanaka and his wife Punha were blessed with a baby girl. She became pregnant the following year, because there was no way they could keep a daughter in the family without trying to conceive a son to be the future heir to his father's estate.

She got pregnant almost at the same time as Haruna, Virimayi's wife, got her first one. They both gave birth to their babies within the same month, with two weeks separating their deliveries, Haruna delivering earlier, both of them delivering boys.

Virimayi's mother had visited her son and daughter-in-law and spent close to a month, and the villagers assumed she had returned to make amends and resuscitate her marriage with Makoni. It amazed her how Makoni had changed to be a responsible and caring husband and father, always jovial and present when his family needed him. Back then when she was his wife, he would not be drawn into discussions that pertained to his family's affairs.

She had also visited Sekai and her husband. Her daughter had a problem of failing to conceive, so she went there on her second visit. "A woman who shares blankets with a man must one day wake up troubled by vomits to signal the presence of a thing in her womb," people in her far away village had loudly said. The mother took her daughter to her people's village to see a gynaecologist. It was then that she came back and conceived, to the happiness of her husband and in-laws.

Makoni was now a respected man in the village and even beyond. He was still a beer drinker just like other men were, but he had adjusted his drinking spree to normal. After a booze he would often go home early. His family would have supper with him. He now had a good herd of cattle in his new kraal and few goats and sheep.

One good night when the moon was rising late, but before they all retired to sleep, he sat with his sons telling them historical stories. His sons knew the importance of knowing their history. A man ought to know who he is and how he came to be what he is.

"In other lands when a woman bears twin-babies, they are all killed." Makoni was in the middle of a history subject.

"Ooh father? Killed? How?" Zvidzai asked, astonishment getting the better of him.

"They would be left in the middle of a vast forest to die of either starvation, cold or could be eaten by wild animals."

"Why is that so?" Matenda politely asked.

"It is an abomination to bear twin-babies. The same applies to triplets."

"What abomination?"

"My sons listen, you children of today ask too many questions. During our time once an event or deed was said to be an abomination you wouldn't ask why. Elders sometimes don't explain everything they say is taboo. Is that the reason why many of you now don't see any sense in such abominations? But still transgressing such set laws would get one in trouble with the angry gods of the land."

"I see." They all chorused as they nodded their heads in agreement. Makoni continued.

"In other lands, albino babies are killed. It is said once you keep them, they bring bad omens to the families."

"What is an albino father?" One of Makoni's younger sons, Manyara, curiously asked.

"Do you know Hoko's third daughter?"

"Musupe?"

"Yes, but that is not her name. Who knows her real name?"

"She is called Revai."

"Yes, Tanaka you know her. Is it because she is a sister to your wife?"

"I knew her before I married her sister."

"It's alright. Back to you Manyara, her real name is Revai as we all heard it from your brother. But the name Musupe is more common than Revai. Do you realise how her skin is?"

"Yes father. She is white, different from anyone, with white eyelashes and chapped skin."

"That's enough Manyara. Only her skin is our concern. A person whose skin is like Revai's is an albino. In our language chiKaranga we call her *musupe*, that is why she got that nickname. So, in those lands people like Revai are killed at birth like I said before."

"But that's unfair and cruel." Matenda empathised.

"If there is anyone who is unfair and cruel then it's their gods. Gods that allow deaths of children they are supposed to protect. If people are obedient to their gods, why do they beget beings that the same gods don't want? Here we have twins and albinos, but our gods haven't abandoned us." Makoni took his walking stick and poked the dying embers of fire with the end that touches the ground when one is walking, to revive the heat.

"Cultures vary from land to land. A culture in one society may not be a culture in another society. These are stories our fathers told us. They used to journey to those lands. They were not like us who are confined in one land. Here in Mposi, very few men have ever gone beyond Pindaufe forest. Their life is around this land of their forefathers, so they think the boundary of Mposi or Munhumutapa is the boundary of the world." Makoni paused, looked up in the sky as if looking for more information from the rising red moon, big and round in complete circumference.

"In other lands, only people of one totem live together as a tribe. There are probably few lands like Mposi where people of different totems are inhabitants. Nehoreka's place is home to the people of lion totem, Shumba."

"What about the Rozvi?"

"Those are Karanga people like us. The word Rozvi used to be a nickname back then. These people are of the heart totem, Moyo. They are warlike masculine men who are notorious for raiding other tribes. The word Rozvi means raider or robber. But the chief who brought those war skills died in a war against the Hungwe whom they defeated by virtue of their numerical superiority. Then his son Dhehwa became chief. Dhehwa was different from his father and predecessor. He incorporated people of other totems into his tribe as long as they accepted the role of being subjects to him. For this reason, Dhehwa was called Bvumavaranda which means Subject-acceptor in chiKaranga."

"Hmmm interesting. Very interesting." His sons spoke with voices of praise to their father.

It was late in the night. The fireplace was cold with no sign of fire but only ashes and dead embers. Makoni stood up and dismissed everyone. Each man took his stool to his hut with smiles beaming in the moonlight. The young men looked like army generals coming from a war of achievement.

Chapter 18

Spring came with its hot sun. After a cold season of winter, every villager did not complain at first. This was time for shelling maize and storing it in granaries. Co-operatives were done here and there with families that were close together, helping each other with small grains like rapoko, millet and sorghum.

Mufakose's wives were seen working cooperatively in community programs because no family did it all alone. Mufakose was never seen participating in any of the co-operatives. Jekanyika was rarely seen with his good old friend who seemed to be giving him a cold shoulder. He had visited him several times but Mufakose was a completely changed man. Even his wives said they felt he was unpredictable and ever dressed in a gloomy mood. A slight mistake would send him into lionish anger that his wives and children feared. Not even Chihera who used to be stubborn was immune from his rage.

One day, Mufakose spotted Runesu going for a hunt. You could not mistake a man going for a hunting expedition by the way he was armed, for he would arm himself like a warrior going for war. Mufakose followed Runesu from afar, making sure he did not see him. On this day, the great hunter was not heading to Pindaufe forest. He was going northwest of Pindaufe. Mufakose kept a reasonable distance between himself and his enemy. For more than an hour, he followed without Runesu knowing anything.

Now Runesu was in the middle of the forest. This forest was not as dense as Pindaufe. A small stream ran through the forest. Besides travellers or hunters, only wild animals drank its water. Runesu was heading downstream into the river. *So, he is looking for water, but he does not have any gourd of water with him*, Mufakose thought to himself.

As one approached the stream, the vegetation changed from ordinary trees that were found everywhere in the forest, to creepers and climbers twisting and weaving themselves through branches. Mufakose thought this was the opportunity he had been waiting for all the past year. He withdrew an arrow from a pocket on his back. Runesu was now in the stream. He found a place with crystal clean water where he could see the bottom of the pool. He checked his surroundings. Mufakose saw it and hid himself behind a big fig tree on the banks of the river.

Runesu made a U-turn and faced the direction from where he came, facing Mufakose (if only he knew he was around). This almost made it difficult for Mufakose to do what he intended to do. Mufakose knew that it was a do or die task, or there was not going to be another chance like that.

Runesu was on all fours now, drinking water as Mufakose watched from afar. He found a gap through the branches of trees and set his arrow on the bow. He pulled it to the limit. Now he watched as Runesu lifted his head after a good intake of water. He aimed, let away the arrow which swiftly went through the air and found Runesu's left cheek. The whole arrowhead sank in his flesh. The great hunter leapt and groaned while trying not to lose his footing.

Runesu withdrew another arrow, quickly set it on the bow and pulled. He aimed but could not certainly satisfy his desire. Runesu was groaning and fighting to pluck off the deadly weapon, but it was not easy. Mufakose let away the arrow that caught Runesu's right eye, blowing it to sap as it entered into his head. Now this was too much for the brave hunter. Still, Mufakose was not done. He withdrew a third arrow, set it on the bow and aimed. This time he caught Runesu's neck piercing through and only the tip of the arrow coming through to the back of his neck. Now three arrows stood on Runesu's body. He groaned helplessly in agony, but Mufakose knew they were far away from the village, so no help would come Runesu's way.

The hunter fell on the ground still branding his weapons that now looked useless. Mufakose came out of the jungle and walked towards Runesu.

"Didn't I tell you? Didn't I tell you that you will never get away with this?"

"Mufa...Mufa...Mu..fakose it's you? The devil!" Runesu was now powerless. Yes, he was a brave hunter but now his enemy had caught him unexpectedly. He hated dying like that in the hands of his enemy. Blood now was trickling from every outlet, natural or not.

"So, you still have the venom to insult me after taking away my wife?"

"Devil, didn't my father pay you back?" His voice grew faint with every word he spoke.

"Scavengers of the jungle will feed on your corpse very soon. Not one of your kinsmen will see your skeleton."

"I don't... Mufakose I don't... kill me then. I tell you kill me now. You will never know peace in this land I...l ...tell you." His last sentence was almost a whisper. Mufakose held his axe up with no mercy. Runesu had no energy to resist. The axe landed on Runesu's head, sinking into his skull. He withdrew it with smears of brain visible on the iron blade. The hunter breathed his last.

Mufakose looked at the dead body of Runesu and spat saliva on it.

"Good! Dog, you are dead. I am done with you. You don't mess with me and expect every day to be business as usual." He beat his bare hairy chest with his fist. One would have thought he was talking to a living man.

After a while, he lifted Runesu's corpse to a deeper pool in that stream. Mufakose laid the body down and headed into the forest then came back after a while. He had tree barks in his hands, which he used to tie a big stone to the body. After that, he pushed the body into the dark pool and watched as the body sank down.

"That's your eternal home now, you animal!" He spoke as he pointed to the sinking corpse.

When the corpse was nowhere to be seen, Mufakose went to where Runesu had been drinking water and bathed himself, thoroughly removing every spot of blood on his body. He also cleaned his axe. He had to be sure that no trace of blood could be seen on him. *Mission accomplished*, he rose and headed home. However, his nostrils were still smelling blood.

It was almost dark when Mufakose entered his homestead. He went straight into his *hozi*, sleeping house without talking to anyone. Normally, he would have first gone to the kraals to check if all his animals were there and in sound health. But on this very day he did not even look in that direction.

"Good evening *Mhukahuru*." This was Chihera with both her knees down punctuating her words with clapping sounds. Mufakose did not reply.

"I said good evening Master."

"Evening." Mufakose mumbled.

"Here is your food."

"No. I am not hungry."

"*Hezvo!* You are not hungry? How is that possible, for you left after we all had breakfast? You did not have lunch with us. So..."

"Woman, stop arraigning me into your court of questions. You heard me well, I am not hungry. Go feed your kids, if they are full give the food to the dogs."

"*Yowee,* is that you Master I am talking to? Did I hear you well?"

"Woman, get away from my sight before I lose my mind! You talk too much. Get out!"

Chihera rose, filled with fright and left. Her co-wives saw her and came to enquire.

"If it does this to a fresh log, what about a dry one? Won't it burn to ashes?" Mufakose's second wife asked, looking worried.

"*Ummmm*, sure an impala cannot tame a wild lion's mood. Neither can the barking of sixteen dogs stop an elephant from rampaging." Chihera said amid fumes.

"Didn't I tell you that his mood is wild, ever since that year Makoni's daughter was snatched from him." Another wife suggested with both her hands on her back.

"This man is childish. What's special about Makoni's daughter that we end up not knowing peace in this homestead? Are we, the five of us not women? We bore him sons and daughters and filled the entire homestead to the brim." The other women laughed except for Chihera who nobody took seriously.

"Women listen, we cannot live in sorrow because of Makoni's daughter Marujata. Tomorrow let's go and confront her straight to her face and tell her to leave our man alone."

Mai Simba said to the other women.

"And how is that of importance to us? Look, Marujata has forgotten about our husband. It's him who still loves another man's wife. Makoni paid him back his wealth including a fine of two heads of cattle on top for time wasted, so how does he still claim that Marujata is his wife?" Chihera reasoned. The other women listened with cocked ears.

"But we just need to show her that we are not cheap women. Five of us combined to be less important than a single lady who got married by a derogatory custom of *musengabere* for that matter. Do you know Mufakose paid everything that my people charged him before him laying a hand on my shoulder? Even you Chihera, Mufakose paid twelve heads of cattle just to ask for your hand in marriage. So, should we stoop low and allow a poor useless lady like Marujata to spoil our marriages? No, that cannot be."

"But Mai Simba has a point. That black-like charcoal daughter of Makoni must be taught a lesson or two."

"So, women, tomorrow when Master leaves the homestead, let's go straight to the western end and see Marujata."

Chapter 19

It was now dark, every woman was busy with her daughters finishing up the cooking, except for a few late cooks who were considered lazy. These would be making fire when other families were having supper. This was a bad habit considering they would finish cooking when their toddlers were fast asleep after a day's non-stop activities.

Young boys had driven their animals back into the kraals, made sure they were closed in securely. Even little girls whose duties were to shut all fowl-runs were done with their tasks.

Runesu had not returned home from the forest. Sometimes he used to come home late particularly when something delayed his return. Marujata was beginning to worry about him. She finished cooking and gave her children food. She did not eat. Her appetite for food had deserted her. Her eyes were now transferred to a path that led out of the yard which her husband always used when coming back home.

"Mother, where is father? Is he sleeping away today?"

"Takunda, what kind of question is that?"

"Mother, we all ate our food, but my father did not eat."

"How is he supposed to eat his food when he is not here?"

"Where is he then?"

"Taku, will you stop bothering me with your silly questions? How am I supposed to know where he is? Next time you can go hunting with your father if you feel you are a man, okay?"

"Yes, I will go with him. Maybe he is carrying something heavy with no one to help him, that's why he is late."

"Be it the way you think, so but stop troubling me with your questions that I have no answers for."

The little boy mumbled something to do with his grandfather and left.

"Where are you going?"

"To my grandfather."

"Come back Taku if you don't want to invite strokes tonight." The boy did not come back. He proceeded with his journey towards his grandfather's huts.

Chivi's huts were in the same proximity that stood Runesu's huts, just like any other homestead. A father's homestead was always flanked by his sons' huts unless the sons were single or only one son had just got married. A short walk led Takunda to his grandfather's *hozi,* sleeping house.

"Is that Taku? Why does your mother send you in darkness like this? Last time I told her that children must not move when it's dark." Chivi was about to enter his house when the sight of Taku stopped him.

"No grandfather, she didn't send me."

"Then what? I can sense you didn't just come for recreation. Come inside and let's talk like men of one totem." Chivi was fond of his grandson. He usually cracked jokes with him, but this evening he saw that the boy was not happy. The old man sat on his stool while the boy sat on the floor with his legs folded, as was the custom.

"Now talk Murambwi. Talk *Mhukahuru.*"

"Grandfather, father is not yet back. I am afraid something might have delayed him. Mother is worried too."

"*Hezvo* Taku! He is not back? This time? How is that possible?"

"Yes grandfather." Chivi was already outside the hut when Taku finished his sentence. He went straight to the cooking hut where MaGumbo, Runesu's mother was. He did not waste time. He ordered his wife to follow him to their son's hut.

"What is it Master? You scare me."

Chivi did not reply. MaGumbo knew him very well. He was a reserved man who could not be drawn into narratives so easily. The old woman followed as their grandson led the way.

"Father, I am sorry I was just procrastinating. I was thinking that I would see him appearing any time now, until your grandson came for you." Marujata managed to explain with a voice of sorrow.

"But Taku said you did not send him."

"Father, you know your grandson is too fast. As an adult I wanted to be certain before I came to you."

"Master, this is not the time for interrogation. Inform other kinsmen and villagers." MaGumbo said with a low voice. Everyone was beginning to worry.

In a short time, the western end of Gokuda village had received news that Runesu who had gone hunting just before noon was nowhere to be seen. Toindepi and Gwenzi, his best friends, were also in the dark. Since morning they had not seen him, the two had told villagers. The entire section of the village was gripped with fear and anxiety. What could have happened to the great hunter? Did an accident happen to him? Did he go to Pindaufe forest? What exactly could have caught up with him?"

All these questions flew from one mouth to another with no answer to each of them. Several groups of men were set up. They started searching for Runesu everywhere they thought a human being could be found. All groups came back empty-handed. Marujata and his mother-in-law MaGumbo were now in sobs.

"People, can my son just disappear in this land where humans move even at night with no harm coming their way? Ooh my gods why have you forsaken me?"

"Women, stop crying. Who told you your son is dead? Why are you wishing him dead?"

"I am not wishing him dead master, so where is he then? Taku my grandson, where is your father? Manyati where is your husband? Please say something that will cool my heart."

MaNyati, as Marujata was called in Chivi's homestead, was all tears. No one could console one another. Even Taku and his siblings, except for the last born who was asleep, looked on, with tears running down their cheeks.

Men woke up at dawn when the *hweva*, morning star, was up and continued with the search. They were good trackers who could tell whose footprints had crossed the areas, coming and going to which direction at what predicted time. Ears were cocked for any sound that could be of help. There was no trace of Runesu. His footprints that were seen from Chivi's homestead towards the forest faded as they went by. No one could tell really where he had gone. Now brave men were chosen to go to Pindaufe forest. This forest was feared by every villager. Only those who volunteered set for the dangerous forest. They spent half the day there and came back without seeing or hearing anything that would please the villagers. Every place was searched from stream, hill, forest, cave, mountain to plain field. Still Runesu could not be found. It was slowly dawning in every villager's mind that the great hunter had seen danger, but to say what kind of danger, nobody had an idea.

That day passed, another day followed, with men searching with the same eagerness, skill and assumptions. Runesu was nowhere to be seen. Now the news spread across the whole Gokuda village and beyond, that Chivi's son had gone missing.

It was on the second day of Runesu's disappearance when men of the western end had gone looking for him that Mufakose's wives got into Runesu's little compound by his father's homestead. Marujata was preparing porridge for her little baby. The women pretended they had not heard of Runesu's disappearance, so they just wanted to see Marujata whom they accused of causing misery in their husband.

"*Vapano!*" Mai Simba saluted the people of the compound. Marujata heard the voice from the back of her mind but did not answer. Mai Simba repeated with the other three women, examining the vicinity of the yard. They had left behind the last and fifth wife in case Mufakose wanted something from them. She was to cover-up for them.

Marujata dashed out of her hut and met her guests. She knew all the women as Mufakose's wives, but what had brought them was something that puzzled her.

"Ooh woman so you are indoors but you decide to ignore our salutation, *hee*?" Chihera was now like a lioness robbed of its cubs by some game. Marujata was taken aback. *What kind of talking is this*, she wondered.

"*Eee* woman, stop causing misery in our family, do you hear me? Our man is not talking to us because of you. Neither is he having food that we cook because you chose to run away from him. Now listen. And you listen very carefully. If this continues, we will come back and snatch you from this Chivi homestead to our place and you become Mufakose's sixth wife."

Marujata was shocked. She remained wide-mouthed with no words coming from her mouth.

"Yes, if that will make our husband happy as before we will grab you by force to his hut. We are done with you." With these words the four left in a huff. Marujata stared at them in confusion.

What are these stupid women up to? Coming to drag me to Mufakose's hut? Under which custom? Have I completely lost my dignity and esteem such that any person can do what they feel like doing? No. I am Runesu's. Even the gods of this land whereupon my feet stand can bear witness to this. So, they actually knew all men of this homestead are not at home, that's why they came to spit venom to my face? Alright, let's see how it will end.

Mufakose saw his wives entering the compound and stopped them. They were in a single file, Chihera heading the little queue.

"Where the hell are you four coming from?"

"From the bush."

"What were you looking for in that bush women, alone?"

"Not very far master. Just beyond those anthills. Rumour has it that Mai Simba's goat delivered three kids, so we wanted to help her look for it and carry the kids and goat home." Chihera was too fast for Mufakose to realise the lies unfolding.

"But you have nothing with you."

"Yes master. The herders actually saw the goat after delivery, it resembles Mai Simba's but it actually is not. We found the owners there busy trying to carry the kids."

"*Ohoo.*" Mufakose nodded but it seemed he felt cheated with Chihera's explanation not sufficient enough to erase his doubts.

Chapter 20

Three days had passed by without anyone knowing anything about Runesu's whereabouts. Terror gripped the entire village and villages nearby. How a man of Runesu's calibre could just go missing for such a long time with no trace of danger that met him baffled every villager. Even Mufakose's four wives who had gone to Chivi's homestead and spoke foul words to Marujata rued their overreaction. It was news all over the community that calamity had hit Chivi's homestead.

On the fourth day, the Chivis set down for a meeting. They wanted to resolve this issue of an omen that had stricken them unexpectedly. Gwenzi and Toindepi were there, even though they were not part of the kinsmen. Every Chivi member knew they were their son's best friends, hence could not be left out.

"We need to consult a diviner. Such matters are beyond our reasoning and understanding." One old man, Mbambo said. He was Runesu's uncle, brother to his father. All members present agreed with him.

"Let's hope my son was eaten by wild animals. Let us not hear that a human being killed him for his jealousy or hatred of him. If that happens, over my dead body his spirit will hunt down every family member of the murderer from the oldest to the youngest. None of them will be spared, mark my words. I will not fold my arms and sit on my haunches while another man cowardly decides to end the life of my son prematurely. I was born and brought up in this community. Ever since my childhood until now, I have not offended anyone. Even so if a man felt I had wronged him or my son wronged him, he should have come forward with his complaint. Being a peace-loving villager, I would have found common ground with him. Where I ought to appease or pay as a solution to redress the situation, I would have obeyed. I swear over the remains of my father and mother that lie side by side on that grey anthill, I will never rest until spiritual justice is served." Chivi pointed in the direction of the family cemetery. Everyone listened attentively to what he was saying slowly, with a tone that carried sorrow. Nobody said anything when he paused. Chivi continued without really looking at his audience.

"Do you people still remember Mufakose's words that year at the Chief's palace? Who was there?"

A few people among the crowd mumbled some sound of confirming their presence at the alleged court.

"Who still remembers what he said? Even the chief was not happy with his words, only that he didn't want to sound like siding with us. Who still remembers that man's words?" Toindepi raised his head.

"Speak, my son. Tell the people."

"Mufakose said no amount of wealth can appease him."

"Exactly. Of course, we took those words lightly, but I am starting to hear them reverberating in my ears like they were said yesterday. Maybe I am being too suspicious, but let me tell you, something in me is telling me that my son did not die of a wild animal bite. He was not that type to be killed without fighting back. The human being who killed him was so smart to conceal every evidence that could lead to his accusation. Now men like us can be outsmarted by a man, but a man cannot outsmart spirits. 'A man's urine can drop as far away from him with all his effort, but the last drop will fall between his legs.' Yes, our people have this proverb."

Everyone at the meeting was shocked to learn that Mufakose was the suspect. "Isn't it he was paid back his wealth with a fine on top?" They asked with fear and shock getting the better of them. Nearly everyone agreed with Chivi except for Taguma, Chivi's young brother who didn't want them to be found guilty of defamation of character. He just wanted to be sure.

"Taguma, my brother, your opinion is not being rubbished away. Yes, we need to be sure, that's why we are going to consult a diviner. But am I saying this out of anger? Can't you see where I am coming from and where I am heading? A man needs to quickly find the head of a snake that has struck once before it repeats. Let us chop the head of the viper before it bites another of us. Am I lying?" Everyone agreed. They said Chivi had spoken well.

Gomwe's homestead was a small compound in Makotore village. It had a few huts, his *hozi*, which was a sleeping house, cooking hut, boys' hut, girls' hut, a granary and a sixth hut that served as his shrine. It was not a magnificent homestead really, but it was neatly maintained. This small homestead was not proportional to his fame. Gomwe himself seemed content with his status. Being a spiritual man who could foresee what the rest of mortal men could not was more important than all human wealth. Was he not more famous than all men who had several wives, children, vast fields and livestock? Sure, he was. Who would not need his service at one given time? All villagers knew his worth, so did the Chivi family.

Mbambo led the Chivi family into Gomwe's homestead. Gomwe's wife received them and directed them into the shrine. They all removed and left behind their footwear away from the doorstep. Each member clapped his or her hands with bowed heads as a sign of respect as they went in.

The inside of the room was amazingly decorated with all sorts of hides of all animals one could think of bones and tusks that the eye could not miss. A man was seated to the right with his legs folded playing the *mbira*, a harp. He was humming a familiar song which Gomwe and his wife would back here and there. An unpleasant and uncommon smell occupied the room, but it would not cause a sneeze.

Gomwe was in his diviner's gear already. Men were ushered to the left while women sat on the right, leaving the upper floor to the host close to where all the diviner's apparatus were.

All of a sudden, Gomwe sprang into the air with the agility of a cheetah. He roared like a bull, like a lion, changing sounds and eventually spoke some words no one understood. For a few minutes he frantically talked to himself. The voice was not his, it seemed. After that he calmed down, now speaking with his known voice, directing his attention to his audience.

"I was about to leave when the spirit stopped me and informed me that there are people coming for consultation here. I saw you in the realm of spirit and I knew what brings you here. Let me hasten and say humans are protected by spirits, but we don't just fold our hands and expect them to do the job. We need to always ask them for protection here and there in our day to day lives as a formality. Several times we tend to tire or overlook that. If you had done the right thing of performing the rite of asking for protection from the gods when going out, you wouldn't be facing this calamity."

No-one said anything. They all nodded their heads in agreement and chorused.

"That's true Great Man."

"Another thing Mbambo and you Chivi, why have you decided to test the spirit?"

Chivi shrunk to the odd question but Mbambo was not moved. Chivi stared at his brother, gathered courage and asked.

"I am sorry Sekuru, did we really test the spirit?"

"Yes, you did. Do you people not know who ate your son?"

"We are not sure Sekuru. We came here as the custom dictates that if a member of a family dies, you consult a diviner for clarification of his or her death."

"Ooh really? There you did the right thing, but still your answer is right. He was murdered. His remains lie in a pool. Yes, I can see his whole body immersed in water but..."

Runesu's mother could not suppress her sorrow. She burst out into a cry.

"Woman this is not a graveyard, it's a shrine. Don't be stupid. Why are you crying like a toddler?"

Other women had to comfort her to silence, but it was not easy. Even men who were known to have the lion's heart were troubled by the revelation.

"Where are my son's remains Sekuru?"

"Mbambo you don't lead the spirit, you follow it. Listen as I narrate. Now you are ahead of the spirit. Should I keep quiet and you finish the last part?"

"No. I am sorry Sekuru. I didn't mean to anger you Sekuru."

"Then listen carefully. Now you know your son was murdered, as you came here assuming and you also know who murdered him. The remains of your son will remain where the murderer ditched them. Just go and invoke your family spirits to fight on his behalf. You know how to invoke the spirits of your ancestors. You will see what will happen in the murderer's family. If he doesn't come forward and confess, the spirits will wipe every human being whose body bears the blood of the murderer. The last to be tormented will lead you to the remains of your son." Gomwe spoke in simple terms, like one reciting a poem of love to a lady. You would not think he was revealing a sorrowful story that had troubled the entire extended family, village and even beyond.

"Yes, the gods are not foolish. Humans always need a diviner amongst them. No human knowledge could have exposed this, for the murderer was very smart, not a single trace of evidence of your son's death can be spotted." All this time Gomwe was saying murderer without really saying out the name of the murderer, though they had all agreed who it was.

Everyone made a heavy sigh of relief simultaneously. A moment of silence crossed the room until Mbambo spoke first.

"Sekuru, your words have been understood. Thank you very much."

"Mbambo, don't be childish. Where on this land have you seen a man thanking a diviner. Even when you leave this shrine don't say goodbye. Neither are you to look back, all of you. You will only bring two heads of cattle the day you see the corpse of your son. Soon after the burial then you drive them here. Understood?"

Mbambo nodded. The others followed suit. Gomwe's wife ushered them out of the hut. As they stood up, the *mbira* from the instrumentalist began, now with a high pitch, for the instrument had been paused when Gomwe was divining. They all left Gomwe's homestead the same way they were told to, until they vanished beyond the vegetation.

Chapter 21

It was now public news that Runesu had died, but no one had seen his corpse or grave. Among villagers who earlier heard about Runesu's missing and subsequent assumed death was Jekanyika, but the idea that his friend Mufakose was the suspect had not sunk in his head. He had viewed villagers' assumptions as biased, citing that they had drawn all assumptions from the fact that the two, Runesu and Mufakose were sworn enemies. "There is a big difference between hating someone and wishing him dead," Jekanyika had argued. Still, the villagers' suspicions grew stronger and stronger with each passing day. One member of Chivi's family, Taguma, had openly told Jekanyika to distance himself from his friend and stop poking his nose into matters that did not concern him. It was then that Jekanyika stopped seeing Mufakose who had actually stopped visiting him, with both men seldom meeting, unlike before Runesu's death. Yes, now people knew he was dead. He was murdered and had not died of animal bite, as had earlier been assumed.

The whole year, Runesu's death became the talk of the village. In the second year, less of his name was mentioned until the news faded in people's memories except for the Chivi family who could not forget. Such is death, close relatives rarely forget.

Time does not stop because there is a crisis or problem among humans. It moves with its pace, in sorrow or happiness. In the second year, everyone was now feeling pity for Marujata. If her husband had died a normal death and was buried, and his spirit brought back into the family, she would have chosen a man for a husband among her husband's young brothers, but alas, Runesu's death was a mysterious one. No grave, no ceremonial rite of bringing in his spirit was done. Normally it was after a year of a man's death that the ceremony of bringing his spirit in the family should be done. After that, his widow was then freed to choose a man for a husband, but only amongst his late husband's relatives.

Only a day passed after the Chivi family had gone to see Gomwe the diviner. On the second day they regrouped for a ritual to be done.

Everyone who was invited amongst relatives woke up early when the morning star, *hweva* was up and bright. This was a family secret. Even those who did not attend were supposed to keep their mouths closed. A handful of people came into Mbambo's homestead and were led by him to the family cemetery. The ritual was to be done at a place adjacent to the graveyard. Mbambo and other elders knew the spot, having visited it a few times to be in communion with their ancestors.

Mbambo ordered others to stay behind as he went to the graveyard where seven graves lay surrounding the grey anthill. He scooped earth from each of the five graves leaving only two which belonged to infants. Earth from graves of adults was the right ingredient of the ritual.

The old man came back cupping the earth with his right hand. He put the soil on the ground and stared at his kinsmen who were in full view of the whole process. Now Mbambo took out his snuff horn and opened it, poured a bit of the product on his left palm and knelt on both knees facing the east. Everybody turned and faced in the same direction.

There was silence. No one spoke. Only actions led the first stage of the ritual. Mbambo then opened his palm and scooped a small morsel of snuff using the two fingers of his right palm. His thumb and pointing finger did the job. He then let down tiny particles of snuff on the earth he had brought from the grave.

"Excuse me Great One. You Murambwi, pass it to Chipamutoro.

Chipamutoro, pass it to Nyaningwe. Nyaningwe, pass it to Nehoreka. Nehoreka, pass it to the next ancestor whom we don't know, in that order until the last ancestor of our people.

We come here as grieved people. What stabbed us unexpectedly is known to you. The enemy who took our son is invincible to us, but vulnerable to you. Let him know that he killed a human being, not an animal. The bones that lay at the bottom of the pool we are yet to know, is your grandson. We implore you to descend on the culprit and cause untold harm to him and his family until he confesses."

Mbambo was sprinkling snuff on the earth as he spoke, until his palm was empty. He then started clapping with his huge palms, sending back echoes of the clapping sounds.

"Ooh yes, Great One, we believe in you. We trust you. You know your grandson did not harm anyone, but the murderer just hated him. Fight back Great One, fight back."

Mbambo finished as others looked on. He then ordered everyone for a last round of clapping that was the final stage of the ritual. They all stood up and headed home quietly in single file. They only spoke to each other when they reached their separation point with each heading to his homestead, which was not far apart.

Although many people no longer spoke about Runesu's death, he remained in the minds of many villagers. Here and there one would feel his absence. That caused the story of his death to be talked about occasionally, but with several different versions.

The Chivis had not told anyone what Gomwe revealed to them. Obviously, Gomwe would not dare disclose such secrets to anyone. He knew his job did not allow him to be of loose heart.

Rumours were part of village life. No one was immune from gossip in any village. Of all gossip, there was this nasty gossip that Gwenzi was seeing Marujata in the cover of darkness. Everybody knew it was an abomination for two unmarried people to be intimate without following the ways of the Karanga people. The gossip had a big section of villagers confirming it to be true. Some would deny whereas others would not ascertain it.

Actually, Gwenzi and Toindepi had visited Marujata one day. Gwenzi had a basket of dried fish that he gave to her as a present. He knew with his friend now dead; it was not easy for his wife and children. Toindepi pledged five big baskets of grains he had barter traded with other villagers. Rumours had it that Gwenzi came back alone at dusk, but his departure had not been noticed.

The Chivis knew their daughter-in-law was a well-behaved woman who knew the ways of their people. Ever since she came into the Chivi family, she had not disappointed them. They knew gossipers were out to tarnish her image. Of course, more than two years was too much time for a widow to remain single, especially a young widow. Nevertheless, Marujata did not indulge in any shameful behaviour.

One day, Gambiza sent a messenger to her daughter Marujata. She did not waste time. As soon as she heard that her mother wanted her home, Marujata set for Makoni in Tseisi village.

"My child, did this rumour that is sweeping across the whole village ever reach your ears?" Gambiza was to say after greetings and having a meal of samp.

"Which rumour, mother?"

"I said did it reach your ears? That's a simple question needing an answer."

"Mother, so many rumours have reached my ears in our village. You know I can't stop people from talking. How can I? Using which custom?"

"Okay let me not beat about the bush. Rumours say you are seeing Gwenzi, your husband's friend."

"*Hezvo*! Mother who told you?"

"As to who told me is not of concern. Answer me first, then we will proceed. "

"No. Not even one day."

"Not even one day, but one moment?"

"Mother it's not true. I am not seeing him, and I swear over my dead husband's bones that lie on a river bedding. I wouldn't do such a thing. Why should I embarrass myself and my people?"

"So, you mean you had not heard the rumour yourself?"

"No mother."

"But your in-laws heard it."

"Heard it? They haven't said anything of that sort. "

"Maybe they are coming any day soon."

"Mother please trust me. I have not seen any man ever since my husband died, trust me."

"It's alright, I trust you but my plea to you is, don't embarrass us. We brought you up in ways of our people. You got married in ways of our people and your husband's family paid everything that your father demanded, so we expect the good behaviour to continue."

Gambiza lowered her voice to almost a whisper and continued.

"You know your husband's family went to a diviner. Now they are waiting for the whole process that the diviner told them to do to come to an end. Then you will be freed. It doesn't matter which year, but you will be freed my child."

"Mother, I don't know what wrong I have done to these gossipers to deserve this. If I was a loose woman, I would have done an abomination with my husband's brothers. They are there. We actually live in one yard. Not one or two of them but they are more than the fingers of both my palms and toes put together, if I were to look at the entire extended family. Not one of them ever said anything shameful to me, nor did I try to seduce one of them. I know my value and dignity." Marujata was now in tears. Her mother felt pity for her. She inwardly blamed herself for asking her. The tone in her daughter's voice was enough to erase her doubts.

Chapter 22

Simba was Mufakose's eldest son by his senior wife. Now he was a man, married with four children. His little home was by his father's homestead. Mufakose had many sons now, seven of whom were married. Nine of his several daughters were married too, having gone to live with their husbands' people. His big homestead was surrounded by his sons' huts, making the huge settlement a big complex. Because Mufakose was rich, all residents of his complex were well fed. All bride prices to all married women of the family were paid to the rightful in-laws in full. Their granaries were always full of grains. Livestock was plentiful in his kraals and pens. Every villager admired the Mufakose family. It was every parent's desire to have them as their in-laws. Of late, the rumours that Mai Simba was a witch and that Mufakose murdered Runesu were the only family let-downs.

One day Simba came home sick. He had gone with other men of his age group to a village co-operative. A neighbour was harvesting his rapoko. It was just after a while of busying themselves that he started complaining of a headache. At first, he thought it was that nagging pain that would soon end, but instead it increased in intensity. He ended up being pulled out of the field to a shade of a tree to take a rest. Still, the pain grew in viciousness. Two friends led him home, left him and returned to work. His wife cooked porridge to which she added a powder generally known to remedy headaches. She gave it to him, but instead of eating he started nose-bleeding. Blood gushed out from the nostrils like it was coming out of a fresh wound. His wife was taken aback. She quickly called all family members who were there.

Everyone tried whatever remedy they could think of, but still the patient did not recover. When the nose-bleeding stopped, Simba said he felt dizzy and powerless. That night he did not sleep. His wife and mother spent the whole night nursing him.

The following day Simba felt worse. Visitors who came to see him would think he was a week-long patient, yet he had become sick only the previous day. From morning to noon, still he was on his mat. Now he could neither walk nor speak. In the evening of that same day, he passed on when the family was organizing a visit to a herbalist.

Simba's death shocked the whole village. He was buried at the family cemetery on the third day of his illness. Villagers as usual started talking in low voices. How he had left a young beautiful wife and young children who needed their father most. How their gods had forsaken them. They went on to say that at least Mufakose was a wealthy man, so his daughter-in-law and grandchildren would not lack. But death is not something that humans are used to.

When a person of Karanga culture dies, after a month of his or her burial, in this case Simba's burial, his people would perform a ritual of comforting close relatives like his wife, children, parents and other family members. The ritual is called *manyaradzo.*

A date was set for the ceremonial rite to be performed. Close friends of the family and neighbours were busy brewing beer and doing everything necessary. Headman Gokuda was informed.

A day before the set day of the ceremony, fate struck in the Mufakose family. Chihera's son who had gone with other herd boys to tend his father's cattle fell from a *munyii* tree and broke his neck and back. His friends carried him home, but he was pronounced dead on arrival. Pandemonium gripped villagers who were busy preparing for the ceremony. The whole event simultaneously turned to a funeral. Humans are not used to calamity, especially death. *How can a healthy boy die just like that? Falling from a tree and dying on the same day? No, this was not normal. What on this land have we done to our gods that cannot be appeased? Ooh we are finished.* Each villager spoke, surprised by the whole event. The most talkative woman Chihera was a pale shadow of herself when this death struck. Villagers found it difficult to console her.

"Ooh my son. Why did they have to take you away so soon? What kind of land never tires from swallowing our children? What kind of gods do not protect their own children?"

Confusion was everywhere in the eastern end of Gokuda village. Even those of the central and western ends were shocked.

The following day the poor boy was laid to rest next to his half-brother, Simba's grave.

Mufakose had begun discussions with his fellow kinsmen concerning the *manyaradzo* ceremony which was aborted due to a funeral that overrode the event. They were speculating whether to start afresh or pause for a while. Just then, two girls from the neighbourhood came running as if something was after their lives.

"Tambu has drowned! Please help, there at the river. Yes, she has drowned!"

Men and women of the family ran to the river with the two girls leading the way. Neighbours also followed.

Tambudzai was Mufakose's daughter with his second wife. The girls had gone bathing in the river as usual. It was before bathing that they started swimming, which they used to do whenever they went to the river as a group. They would play aquatic games in the waters of the pool. It was then that Tambudzai drowned.

The crowd reached the river quickly. They spotted the body floating on top of the water like a log near the rocks. Everyone was shocked. How a grown-up lady like Tambudzai would drown in waters that went as high as one's chest was baffling. Why she had drowned on that day when they used to swim in that same pool ever since they were young girls was astonishing. The river had no crocodiles. This was pure drowning.

Two men jumped into the water and retrieved the body to dry ground. Sure, the body was lifeless. Her belly was bulging.

"Poor girl, she took in too much water!" Villagers exclaimed. Their hearts could not bear the sight of a dead body lying before them. Another young life lost again. You wish a human being had a spare life such that if the first life dies you replace it with a spare one immediately.

Tambudzai's corpse was carried to the village. Every villager was speechless and powerless. Tears trickled from their cheeks like toddlers. The entire eastern end of the village now looked like a funeral parlour. Who had the strength to lead a song of comfort? Who had a voice to ask the person standing next to him or her what it all meant? Who had answers to such tragedies that befell a single family in a space of a single moon? It was beyond human understanding. But all villagers concluded that something was amiss.

Mufakose had two brothers, Gwavuya and Rindai, whose homesteads were within the same village. Just a stone's throw away was Gwavuya's homestead to the south of Mufakose's. An outcry was heard from Rindai's homestead to the east. Their families were among the mourners.

The Karanga people do not allow children at funerals. They leave them behind when going for a funeral. If a funeral is at home, children are transferred to a homestead of the next of kin.

Tambudzai's corpse would be laid to rest the following day. Everyone was preparing for the burial when a woman came running. A little boy had died of food choking, she narrated amid sobs. The lady was Mufakose's niece who lived with his younger brother Rindai, and the poor boy was Gwavuya's son. This was shocking indeed. How was that possible? Food choking a boy to death? "What food?" Everyone asked. The children were eating cold sweet potatoes leftover from the previous night. Villagers were confused.

Tambudzai's body was buried that day and the following day they buried the little boy's body.

Gwavuya was not that lucky in terms of children bearing. The majority of his children were female. He had only three sons, two from his first wife and one from his third and last wife. His second wife had given him daughters only, something he openly despised. Actually, he felt not man enough with just three sons when his other brothers had several of them. The boys came late in the family such that they were too young for them to know what was going on concerning issues of the family.

Mourners were now coming home from the family cemetery when a word from a herd boy was heard. Four hyenas had attacked goats that belonged to Gwavuya in broad daylight. The three boys fought it but two of them were unlucky. The dangerous wild animals gnawed them to death after a fierce fight. The other boy, who was the youngest, survived by climbing into a tall tree where he watched his brothers being killed, without managing any help. His cowardice saved his life.

"What exactly is happening in this village? What wrong have we done to the gods of this land? Not a day passes without us burying one of us. Who knows who is next?"

Villagers were caught with fright. Even their shaky voices revealed their horror. During the night, they began blocking their doors with huge items like mortars and put their weapons close by, in case harm might visit them. No villager would have a peaceful night's sleep. One would thank the gods if at all they woke up alive.

The bodies of the two boys were tattered from the wounds of the beasts. One corpse had its belly ripped open and intestines hanging out, while the other had a broken skull. The sight of the two corpses were not for the faint-hearted. Few women came close to them.

Before the burial, Rindai whose sons were killed by the hyenas summoned every member of the Mufakose family to a meeting.

"My people, I am really saddened by these events where our children are mysteriously dying. I know you are also saddened, but you have no guts to stand up and speak out. Now let's speak as people of one family. We cannot fold our hands like this when death has found residence among us. We don't know who is next. I know before or after laying these two, we will receive some news of death again. Mysteriously too. Where in this land have you heard that hyenas attack humans during the day? No, let's not sit and relax."

"What do you suggest we do?" Gwavuya asked. Mufakose was quiet with his face bowed down.

"Of course, we must visit a diviner."

"For what?" Mufakose asked with a high-pitched voice.

"Why do you ask such a question? Don't you see this is beyond human knowledge? Alright, tell us what you suggest we do." Gwavuya queried. It was a heated meeting with tempers rising here and there. Accusations and counteraccusations. Everyone wanted their opinions to be respected and observed.

The meeting was interrupted by Gumhai, the Chief's messenger. They had to stop and listen to him. Every villager knew that once Gumhai stepped in your yard, it meant he had some news that demanded attention.

Chapter 23

The two boys' bodies were buried in the evening. The following day at dawn, they set off for the Chief's palace. Gumhai had told them that the Chief wanted their presence in the morning.

He had also gone to see the Makonis who the Chief wanted as witnesses. Only the Chivis were left out.

"I remember you once came here some years ago, but I can't remember which year it was exactly." Chief Mposi started, in a low hoarse voice when the court hearing began, but the voice was audible. Old age was now taking a toll on him. Even his strides when walking revealed that he was now very old. Standing up was of big concern, the same applied with his sitting down.

"It was an issue concerning Chivi's son who had taken Makoni's daughter to be his wife, yet her father had married her off to Mufakose when she was young. You all know the story I am sure." The crowd before the chief and his judiciary nodded in confirmation.

"Ooh yes, you have to recall the story if an old man like me can still vividly remember. Now I will not dwell on every detail of the story as you all know the story." Chief Mposi coughed to clear his throat and continued.

"On that day, the verdict of the court was that Makoni must pay back what Mufakose gave him, with a penalty on top for time wasting and breaking our cultural laws. I eventually heard that Makoni did exactly that, am I right?" Everyone nodded.

"But before that, Mufakose said something that did not go down well with this court, though we did not show it. We feared you the people of Mposi community would have said the Chief was biased. Mufakose said something to do with his dissatisfaction with whatever wealth Makoni was to pay him back. I want someone to repeat his words here for the benefit of those who were not here or for those that might have forgotten." Chief Mposi raised his crowned head and searched the crowd with eager rolling eyes.

"Can someone repeat the words?" Zenda stood up and saluted the entire court then proceeded.

"He said, 'no amount of wealth is going to appease me.'"

"Ooh, thank you Zenda. You are a wise man. Sit down." Zenda sat down and paid attention, just like the rest of the audience.

"Now listen, all of you. When we passed that verdict, we took into consideration that Makoni's daughter was already pregnant by Chivi's son. Besides the pregnancy, she was already made a wife by the same son of Chivi. How were we going to reverse that? When we try cases here in this court, we follow the ways of our people. No case is new in this community. Every crime has a way of redressing it so that people live together in peace. Now Mufakose, stand up!" Mufakose stood up immediately.

"What did you do to Chivi's son?"

Mufakose hesitated.

"Mufakose, am I talking to myself? If so, then I am mad. What did you do to Chivi's son?"

"Which son of Chivi are you talking about, *Mhukahuru*?"

"Which other son of Chivi must we bring in, in this context? The one who took away your wife! Where is his corpse?"

"*Mhukahuru*, how am I supposed to know that?"

"It's alright, but how is it that an old woman disappears and suddenly a hyena vomits grey hair? Is it a coincidence?"

"*Mhukahuru*, of all people of this community, why are you accusing me?"

"Don't ask me questions. Answer me. Didn't you say you won't be appeased by any kind of wealth to accept the verdict I passed here that year? Mufakose, we were not born yesterday. These grey hairs you see in everyone's head are no fluke, we are old people. Not only old, but wise too. Do you think what is happening in your family is normal? Where in this land have you heard that death occurs each and every day in a single family? It's alright, you shall see if you think a man can die like a fly and life goes back to normal. I thought with the status and respect you are commanding in this community, you are wise. You are such a stupid cruel man. See now how you have thrown the entire family in hot soup. Spirits are not humans for you to...."

"But *Mhukahuru*..."

"Shut up! You don't open your cave when I am talking. Shut up! You, his kinsmen."

The Chief turned to Mufakose's kinsmen.

"You are equally foolish. Why do you want the whole family to be wiped away because of one man's sin? Why don't you rise up and revolt against him? You fear his big name? It's the big name that has been cast onto a dog. He does not deserve it. A family man who does not watch his behaviour always brews troubles for his family." The chief was now angry. His commanding voice was now very high, even a passer-by could hear it.

"Today I did not call you here to try you, but if a father in a family sees children quarrelling among themselves, does he not intervene? If he doesn't intervene, is his name not going to be soiled? It's equally shameful and tarnishes the image of the entire community. If one rotten berry is in the same basket with good ones, the whole basket ends up being spoiled. Mufakose, you have no respect for human life. Neither do you have respect for the gods of this land. Yes, we will do nothing to you, but the spirits will haunt you forever until such a day you confess your sins."

People were dismissed. Yes, they were arraigned before the Chief's court, but it was not a usual court of interrogations and accusations.

The Makonis took their way back home while the Mufakoses went theirs. Along the way, arguments began as the majority of them suggested they call a diviner. Mufakose was against the idea. A few members sided with him.

"Ever since I was born, and now I am an old man, I have never heard of a man who fears the sight of a diviner. Is he not there to reveal something that is beyond human understanding?" Gwavuya asked.

"And you think those people know everything right? Are they not mortal like us?" Mufakose was still against the idea of going to see a diviner.

"Brother, since when have our people overlooked the works of diviners? Our forefathers used to consult them, and it is this custom that we grew up knowing, that if a calamity befall us, we call or visit them. Is there anything new here?" Mufakose did not reply Gwavuya. He kept moving as if nothing had been said.

"Normally, a man who dreads the consultation of a diviner knows he is guilty." Rindai was bold enough to speak out.

"Brother, are you also accusing me of something?" Mufakose looked at Rindai straight in his eyes.

"I am not accusing you of anything, but do not deny the consultation of a diviner when the entire family is stared by death like this. You know I lost two sons just two days ago, now you are being thick-headed and refuse advice."

"Is this an insult or what?"

"Whatever you call it but going to see a diviner is what the family will do. You said no amount of wealth is going to appease you when Makoni paid back everything, now Chivi's son died a mysterious death. Who do you want the people of this community to accuse? Didn't our elders warn us that we should be careful with what we mouth? A word said is irreversible. Even if Chivi's son was killed by someone else or a wild animal, but as long as they haven't seen the murderer, they will always accuse you. Match that with deaths that are occurring every day in our family. Can't you see it's an evil omen? It's the spirit of the dead man killing us." Gwavuya puffed, now foaming on both sides of his mouth.

Mufakose was shell shocked. He was not used to being challenged by his kinsmen. He was the wealthiest of all his brothers, so they worshipped him since they would many times need his help. Mufakose was not a generous man, but he would help a kinsman on condition that in turn they did something for him. It was usually these situations that led his relatives to not challenge his decisions no matter how wrong they were.

Their discussion was interrupted by three men whom they met. They were men from the eastern end of the village. They had bad news. A woman of the Mufakose family who was heavy with pregnancy had endured prenatal complications. Both mother and unborn baby died. The two midwives who were there could not save their lives. The woman was Gwavuya's wife. Gwavuya who had been the most vocal in their discussions. The one who had boldly challenged him and questioned his refusal to participate in such a sensitive issue that demanded their togetherness.

"Ooh my wife! My child! Didn't we tell you brother? Didn't we? Didn't the chief tell you? Confess! Please confess before we all die." The big old man cried loudly like a kid stung by a scorpion. The news hit the procession of travellers like a spear of death branded by the devil. Fear gripped them all.

Mufakose kept quiet. You could not tell what was going on in his head.

Chapter 24

The baby's body was not to be buried by every villager. Neither was it buried at the village cemetery. It was buried by the riverside. According to Karanga culture, if a baby dies before germinating teeth, its body is buried by old women at the riverside.

The Mufakose family sent a word to their in-laws, informing them of the death of their daughter. They were shell-shocked and as unforgiving as Karanga parents could get. After exchanging strong words, the messenger eventually convinced them to attend the funeral. The Mufakoses had no issues with their in-laws. Mufakose was by far one of their best sons-in-law, having paid full rovora, a gesture that pleased them.

Finally, the woman's body was laid to rest. The in-laws left immediately after the burial. They had heard of the deaths taking place in their son-in-law's family and did not want to be part of it.

Gomwe was known as a diviner by the whole community and even beyond. Other than being a diviner nothing more was he known for. Villagers could often define the words Gomwe and diviner with the same meaning with each substituting the other in conversations. You would not blame them because they knew no other diviner besides Gomwe. Of course, it was once thought Hoko was also a diviner, but it was later learnt he was just a rainmaker.

Many a time, villagers would visit Gomwe's shrine for consultation. But sometimes, for special cases he would go to his patients' homes too. That is what Gomwe did with the Mufakose family, because their problem involved a number of people.

"Dembai! Dembai can you hear me?"

"Yes father, I am here." The little girl came running like a whirlwind.

"Go to the cooking hut and be given a calabash of water and a cup by your mother. Your mother forgets that today I am on a journey." The girl had already gone by the time Gomwe finished his last sentence, making it look like he was talking to himself.

In a short while, the girl came carrying the calabash too full of water splashing out of the container onto her body. Her father helped her bring the calabash down. She took the cup made of gourd plant, fetched a cupful of water and gave it to her father.

"Dembai, which hand is that one? How many times must we tell you that you don't give or receive something from an adult using your left hand?"

"I am sorry father."

"Next time you repeat the same mistake, I will pull those deaf ears of yours."

After bathing, Gomwe got into his shrine and took his skinbag which was already loaded. His instrumentalist was to accompany him. Only the two of them were enough for the job.

The Chivis were there. The Makonis were there. All villagers informed, from western and central ends were there. They all flocked to a big open space just adjacent to Mufakose's homestead, which was reserved for *jenaguru*, full moon festivals. The majority of the people were those who were not invited. They wanted to see how it would end. They were scattered here and there like shepherd-less sheep.

The appearance of Gomwe and his man drew everyone's attention. All eyes were on them as they approached the Mufakose yard. They were received by elders of the family who ushered them into one of the many huts haphazardly spread across the yard. They had a small meeting in low voices.

After that, they all headed to the open space where everyone was gathered. A small arena on the centre of the space was formed to act as a platform for the diviner.

Hoko, headmen Gokuda and Tseisi were some of the respected guests. They sat on their stools and watched the proceedings quietly. The rest of the crowd were seated on the ground.

Gomwe started his job with a common and familiar song *Gona raMachingura rapedza hama.* His instrumentalist brought the *mbira* to a matching tune. So soothing and melodious were the lyrics that when the harp went to a high pitch some people stood up to dance. Gomwe was a good dancer too, and in fact one of the best.

Suddenly amidst the song, he leapt into the air like a huge cat that had stepped on hot embers of the fire. He galloped in that direction and galloped in the other. He roared like a lion charging towards game. The instrument continued. The dancers were so good in their game that even watchers enjoyed the spectacle. You would not think this was a troubled village.

Usually, children were forbidden from gathering that had to do with spiritual matters, but on this day all Mufakose family members were there as according to the diviner's order. Gomwe beckoned his man to stop the harp. People returned to their seats.

"Can you people seated in here in front move backwards." Gomwe ordered. The front row of people fidgeted backwards. Some were reluctant, but a repeat of the same statement of emphasis brought the section of the crowd to the right requirement.

"Now, all Mufakose family members come and sit here before me." They obeyed. Mufakose himself was the last and sat at the end of that group close to the rest of the crowd.

Gomwe reached in his skinbag and brought out a concoction that he put in a clay basin.

"Bring some water for me please."

In a short while, water was given to him. He mixed the powder and water in full view of the crowd and stirred. After that he took a wildebeest tail and dipped it in the same stuff and sprinkled every Mufakose family member. He dipped again and repeated the sprinkle. On his third sprinkle one of the youngest girls burst into a sudden cry. It was like a cry of one tormented by something. The girl rose from her feet and cried loudly. Other adults who were seated close by tried to force her down.

"Leave her! Leave her!" Gomwe commanded.

"Yes, it's you whom I wanted. Now two spirits have locked horns. Who are you?"

The little girl shook her head and spread her arms like a wrestler about to pounce on an opponent. She beat her chest hard and puffed as she charged forward. People gave her way. She moved towards Gomwe coming face to face with him, a metre separating the two. Everyone knew she was in a trance.

"Who are you? Speak out!" Gomwe barked.

"Why do you ask me who I am? You know me. Everyone here knows me." It was a male voice, so unmistakably male. It was a familiar voice.

"Who are you and how can I help you?"

"What is my enemy doing here?"

"Now you ask me another question. Anyway, who is your enemy?"

"He is here. Yes, the one who killed me is here."

"Alright, can you locate him?"

The little girl turned and faced the row of people where her family were seated.

"Go ahead, reach for the person."

The girl made steps forward through the crowd straight to where Mufakose was seated. She bolted there and stared at him with red piercing eyes. Mufakose felt uneasy and fidgeted frantically like a toddler with boils on his buttocks. Still, the girl remained rooted on the spot like a statue.

"Brother, tell your daughter to leave me alone. I know both of you, father and daughter hate me."

"Mufakose shut up! How can a young girl of this age hate a grown man like you? For what reason?" Gomwe intervened.

"Alright young girl, we have seen your enemy indeed. Can you people see the man who is causing all the deaths you saw these past days?" A big chorus of 'yes' swept across the crowd.

"Now spirit, tell us, who are you?"

"I told you, you know me. My father is here. My mother is here. My wife is here. My children are here, and all my people are here."

"But still, people don't want a clue. Be clear and say out your name. Who are you?" Gomwe pressed on. The spirit upon the girl hesitated.

"I am Runesu." A huge sigh of astonishment filled the sky.

"Runesu who?"

"Runesu Chivi, of course!"

A loud cry was heard from a woman. It was Runesu's wife, Marujata. Another cry answered the sorrowful sound. Now it was his mother. The two women were dragged out of the crowd for calmness to prevail. They were sent to the homestead still crying. They watched the proceedings from there.

"So, all these years you've known where I am, but you never informed my people?" The voice accused the diviner.

"That is why I invoked your spirit. Now you can tell your people where you are. Where is your body lying?"

"Down in waters."

"Which waters?"

"In Gwenhoro river."

Everyone was open-mouthed with palms covering their mouths. All pairs of eyes were on the drama with cocked ears.

"Can you lead us to the pool?"

"Sure."

"Can I have ten brave men to accompany us to the stream?" Gomwe requested. More than ten men volunteered. Some of them were turned down to reach the exact requirement.

The girl led the way. The rest of the crowd remained behind. The little girl got into a sprint as soon as she left the crowd. The men followed in close pursuit. She increased her sprint to a fast run with men close by.

In a short while, they reached the stream. The girl dived into the pool and came back after a few seconds holding a human skull. She swam to dry ground and place it there. It was a broken skull. She swam back, deep in the water and brought out ribs with both hands. Obviously, these were ribs that made up the rib cage. All men stood aloof and watched in perplexity. She swam to dry ground again and laid the bones next to the skull. She frequented the route bringing a bone or two from under water in that same order, until all bones were retrieved from underneath the water.

A man was sent back to the village to collect a big skinbag. When he returned, all bones were deposited into the skinbag. There was no flesh or tendon on the bones, just clean white bones.

Chapter 25

It was now noon. The crowd saw the diviner and his helpers coming back. Those who were up rushed back to their places and sat down. Curiosity was the order of the moment.

"Here is the body of your son that Mufakose killed. Do you hear me, the Chivi family?" Gomwe said to the Chivi family. A low murmur of confirmation came from a section of people where the Chivis were.

"Now I am done with my job. I have shown you the murderer of your son and where his body laid all these years. Now you can make arrangements for his proper burial."

Gomwe went into the Mufakose's compound and undressed himself from his diviner's attire, put on his usual clothes and came back. He and his instrumentalist bade them farewell and left.

The little girl who was possessed by Runesu's spirit was now normal. She seemed to have no idea of everything that she had said and done. She was actually surprised when all eyes were on her.

Mbambo rose up and lifted the big skinbag which had Runesu's skeleton and gave it to the Mufakose family.

"This is your body. You ate all the flesh like lions, now you can do what you want with those bones." He turned and ordered his people to leave the place. They obeyed. A procession of the Chivis was seen leaving the Mufakose homestead. The Mufakoses and other villagers knew what it meant.

The Mufakose family had to put their heads together despite their anger and hatred towards their kinsman who had thrown them into hot soup.

The following day they visited Gomwe's shrine.

"The spirit speaks through that girl. Let her say what really is supposed to be done. I am coming tomorrow to invoke his spirit." That was what Gomwe said to the Mufakose family.

Two days passed as the bones of Runesu lay in their home. Sorrow dwelt in every quarter of their homesteads during those days.

On the third day as he promised, Gomwe came to do his job. The family gathered again. The girl Runesu's spirit spoke through was brought forward. A single song and sprinkling of herbs brought her to a trance again.

"Now tell us, we brought you to your people, but your people surrendered you to the family of your murderer so that they make an atonement for your murder. What must they do?"

"They must pay my people with thirty heads of cattle and a virgin girl for a wife. The wife should be given to one of my brothers as a wife. If the wife bears a son, they call him Runesu, so that my name will not be extinct. Once the cattle and lady are with my people, then they can lay me to rest. The rest of the custom follows as usual. Have I made myself clear?"

Everyone present nodded to the commanding male voice. When a spirit speaks mortal men listen with no objections.

Of the three Mufakose brothers, two of them pledged five heads of cattle each. The remainder of twenty cattle was pledged by him, Mufakose. They had to be fast. They could not bear the burden of storing the bones of a non-relative in their compound. The other issue that took time to debate was the issue of a virgin girl which the spirit had demanded. Whose daughter was going to be forced into such a marriage as atonement to a wrong a father did? Mothers were especially unwilling to part with their daughters in that fashion. Of course, the custom was known across the entire community of Mposi, but it was scoffed at. Wherever the lady chosen would be seen, people would say "there is the lady who was used as water to extinguish a homestead on fire. There is she, the lady of atonement." No girl would like that treatment either.

Gomwe helped them choose the rightful girl. He chose the girl who was possessed by the spirit of the dead man. The girl belonged to Mufakose's brother, the outspoken one. Her mother was against the idea, just like all mothers would have done were it that their daughters were chosen. The whole family grouped together and persuaded her.

"You know your daughter has been possessed by the spirit of this man for two days now. You know what our people say would happen if you deny her being sent to the Chivis. You would rather have her alive in the Chivi family than her dead in your home. You can object to what humans say, but you cannot object to what spirits say, right?"

"But it's you who chose my daughter, not the spirit."

"Yes it is, but spirits are watching over from their dwelling places, don't you know that? See, how the spirits located the remains of a man who died some years ago? Are they not conscious of everything that happens in this universe?"

The woman was cornered. *They speak sense*, she concluded. As *long as she is alive, after all she was going to marry at any given time in her future. I am sure the Chivis are going to be good in-laws*, she added in her thoughts.

The following day all thirty heads of cattle were driven to the Chivis. The virgin girl was in front dressed like an adult bride, carrying a gourd of fresh beer. She led the animals that followed her without making any effort to run away. The Mufakoses were at the back.

They were received by the Chivis. The cattle were put in a kraal and the girl and her family ushered into a big hut. The whole Chivi family was there. Chezhira, who had come all the way from Masarira village, was there too. Now she was a big grown-up woman with three children whose ages were a year or some months separate in-between. She was a good woman who knew her duty was to expand her husband's family, her husband's people said. Her first-born child was a boy, which was very much praised as having born an heir to her husband.

They were still good friends with Marujata. They often visited each other.

The event of handing over the wealth to the Chivis did not take long. That very day, Runesu's remains were buried at the family cemetery just like other relatives who had passed on. Gomwe was given his reward for a stern job. The Mufakoses also paid him for helping settle one of the most troubling misunderstandings between two families. The girl from the Mufakose family was given to Runesu's brother, the youngest by their mother. She was to grow up as his wife in that family. If ever the chosen boy was to marry later in life, then his wife or wives were to be his second or third wives. This girl was already the senior wife and would remain so.

Marujata was happy to be set free, after years of celibacy. She knew it would not take long for her to marry because already one of her husband's brothers was showing affection towards her. They had had conversations with their eyes that only the two knew what it meant. A few relatives also suspected them. The good part was that both of them were waiting for the right time. And now was the time.

Two days after the burial of Runesu's remains, villagers of Gokuda and other villages were expecting peace to prevail. This kind of situation they had seen themselves was unusual and no one could get used to it. Who could be used to suffering, deaths and mourning?

The Chivis were led by Mbambo to that same spot they visited by the cemetery side to thank their ancestors on the atonement of the death of their son.

They returned home, but their hearts were still in pain for losing their son. It was as if Runesu had passed on within that week of the burial of his remains. But sometimes one has to accept that a life lost is never gained.

The same week in the middle of the night, people of Mufakose woke up to shouts from every quarter of the yard. Mufakose's *hozi*, main house, was on fire. Flames of fire were blazing high in the sky like a veld burning. People tried to extinguish the fire with whatever means they could think of, to no avail. Pandemonium gripped the crowd that had gathered to assist. In a short time, the roof fell in with flames raging.

"What triggered the fire? Where did it all start from?" No one could answer the questions. People were now standing far away watching, seeing everyone was now sure they had lost the fight.

"Where is Mufakose when his house is burning like this?" It was then that everyone saw that Mufakose was not among people in the crowd. It dawned in everyone's head that something was not alright.

It was almost in the early hours of the morning that they smelt an unpleasant smell from one corner of the house. One brave man took a big stick and poked in the corner. What he saw shocked him. He took a step backwards and beckoned others to help him see.

"Are my eyes deceiving me? Is this not the body of a human being?"

Two more men took a stick each and poked the debris piled on the corner. Sure, it was a smoked body of a human being defaced beyond recognition. However, the legs were still not burnt. Just a thorough look at his body, one could easily know it was him, Mufakose.

His wives were called to explain who had spent the night with him, which they all said he was alone in his room throughout the night.

Two versions of the death of Mufakose became public news that day. Some suspected his brothers of foul play. Others said he had committed suicide. Nonetheless, nobody cared really about his death, not his children nor his wives. The following day his remains were laid to rest.

After a year, his wealth was shared equitably between his two brothers. All his livestock, wives and children were also given to his brothers. No beer was brewed to bring back his spirit into the family, because it was concluded that he had committed suicide.

THE END

Lightning Source UK Ltd.
Milton Keynes UK
UKHW010920160522
403010UK00003B/48